W
SIGNIFICANCE

July 2016

To Bill Calpus,

Lifetouch is a company whose significance in so many lives is immeasurable — and you, with humility and strength, have helped the Lifetouch wings to open wide and fly far. I guess you must be right where you are meant to be.

With appreciation and admiration,

Donna Tartar Musselman

WINGS OF SIGNIFICANCE

DONNA TARTAR MUSSELMAN

TATE PUBLISHING
AND ENTERPRISES, LLC

Published by Tate Publishing & Enterprises, LLC
127 E. Trade Center Terrace | Mustang, Oklahoma 73064 USA
1.888.361.9473 | www.tatepublishing.com

Tate Publishing is committed to excellence in the publishing industry. The company reflects the philosophy established by the founders, based on Psalm 68:11,
"The Lord gave the word and great was the company of those who published it."

Book design copyright © 2016 by Tate Publishing, LLC. All rights reserved.
Cover design by Joshua Rafols
Interior design by Richell Balansag

Published in the United States of America

ISBN: 978-1-68207-022-2
1. Fiction / Hispanic & Latino
2. Fiction / Fairy Tales, Folk Tales, Legends & Mythology
16.01.21

To my life-enriching sons, Bret, Greg, Bart and Kirk, and their families. Thanks for beautiful memories, for cherishing nature with me, sharing exciting pursuits of the awesome bald eagle, and for your beautiful photography, Bret, Greg, Kirk, and Bart's son, Alyn. A special thanks to Bret for his photographic expertise and dedication. America's noble winged symbol of freedom has made a healthy comeback, thanks to caring, informative places like the National Eagle Center in Wabasha, Minnesota, and the Nisqually National Wildlife Refuge in Washington's Puget Sound.

1

It was an ordinary day in the mountain valley—seemingly like others before it, but truly unique unto itself. What is a day, after all, but a capturing together in the stillness of its seconds all things unique unto themselves and in constant motion, with change so continually ongoing it appears in the form of stability? Everything is in its place. As it is meant to be.

Think of it. In ordinary seconds, violence and peace embrace, producing new life and death as relentlessly as a waterwheel churning a still river into scattered droplets, only to blend them once more into the whole. High in the universe, far beyond where the eagle flies, a fire rages. Feeding frenetically upon itself, it spews a constant rain of hot danger toward the valley. The way is long, and along the way the anger cools, dissipates, fans out, and learns to laugh and dance through frothy clouds. It lights but a warming gleam on the oil the eagle has spread with her beak throughout the feathers that form her outstretched wings.

She rests, thus adorned, on what might appear to be nothing at all but in fact is a pillow, air currents gathered together. Just to hold her aloft. Alone, there is nothing…together, all…whispering…humming …singing…Shouting.

On this ordinary day, at the valley's edge, tall pines sipped nourishment from countless drops of brisk water that gathered into a ribbon of motion, bouncing, skating toward the ocean. Small rocks and dirt and clay and bits of pine had laid the path, trickling in a narrow slither of drops that had joined on their way down from the top of the tallest mountain. She was the mountain mother, the only one within this range adorned with combinations of pine and boulders, rocks and scrub, lavender and yellow blooms. The others varied in height and breadth, some lush with green, others barren and rock-strewn. Reaching out to one another, each as it was, they formed together a protective circle all around the valley.

So it seemed, as always, on that late summer morning that everything was in its place, gathered in discordant harmony, working together, even unintentionally, to create the ageless scheme of change, and constancy, and purpose. As it was meant to be.

None seemed aware that strange new forces were gathering on that ordinary day, bringing change more explosive and far-reaching than any there in the quiet valley ever could have known or foreseen.

Even the large boulder, nestled low and helping to shore up the mountain's side, saw himself as a vital part of the massive whole, impervious to the mysterious force causing thin rivulets of sand to skip across him. His long, flat body brilliantly streaked with sulfite and flecked with gold, he had always been the natural choice, the only boulder on the mountain mother to have served as a fitting throne to the grand family of eagles that nested above him year after year through many ordinary days. He was preparing now to provide a dependable landing pad for the season's only surviving eaglet, unwittingly about to grab his very first scoop of air.

The young male had been practicing, aiming his gaze intently down toward the boulder as he opened and closed his wings, testing the play of the wind through his feathers as it cast him, lifted him, left him hanging cautiously over the huge aerie that stretched across sturdy branches high up on a birch tree.

When the time came, the eaglet would be well-prepared for his moment. More than four months ago, his parents had reinforced their nest, building it anew with fresh moss and sticks and branches. Faithfully, they had warmed their lofty home, nurturing in turn, gracing it with new life, then bringing new death, as needed, to fill the young crops again and again. By fulfilling their own destinies, they prepared him for his.

No ordinary eaglet, the young male had somehow worked his way to the edge of the nest days before he would be deemed ready by his parents. This young raptor did not do things according to expectations. In his earliest days, he had been the smallest in the nest. He had had to draw on every ounce of his strength just to survive, stretching his wobbly neck to push his head up stubbornly between the others, then higher, beak always wide open, ready to receive every morsel of sustenance his parents could provide. Eventually, he was the strongest eaglet in the nest. Then one day, he was the only one. His two siblings had not survived.

He had learned early how challenging life could be. But so exciting! Here he was, right on the edge of the huge nest, out of the warm security of its center on his own, before his mother had even had the chance to stir him out for his dizzying lesson in flight.

She and her mate had been drawn away to circle the valley together, not in their usual teamwork of the hunt, but to seek out the cause of the unfamiliar, a strange presence moving, rumbling ever louder toward them. Usually, one of them stayed close, attending to the noisy demands of their still-downy young.

But there was something different on this day, something ominous, invasive coming. They could feel it. The hen had followed her mate away from the nest to investigate.

The noise in the distance grew louder. At the same moment, the tree that was home to the eagles trembled, almost imperceptibly. The young tiercel had been leaning too far forward and wobbled precariously on the edge of the nest, barely holding on.

From a distance, his mother detected his unsteadiness and screamed out a warning. Breaking away from the shared circle of flight, she streaked toward him, "Aeeeehh!" she cried. "Get back *in* the nest where you are safe!"

But the young male was again aiming his gaze intently down toward the glistening boulder, again leaning into the wind, again opening his wings to the thrill of the lift.

Reluctantly, he closed his wings and sank back into familiar safety.

"Eeoooww!" called his mother. "Good, don't move! Stay there! Wait for me, I am coming to you!"

Perhaps to tease her, or to show he could do it, the brash young bird stepped up again and leaned forward just a bit farther than he had before. Suddenly, the tree was trembling again, as the earth shook beneath it. This time the eaglet had ventured too far! He lost his grip and tumbled forward, hurtling helplessly through the air, bolting down toward the boulder. There was nothing to grab onto, no way to stop—no time for his mother to swoop beneath him and break his fall.

His father saw it happening and turned sharply back toward the nest, calling out, "Eeeaaahhh! Just allow yourself to fly! Don't fight the air. Let go of your fear! Allow your wings to work for you as they are meant to do. You were *made* to fly!"

Responding to his father's call, the young one managed to thrust his novice wings out from his flailing body again just a little more. As if to help, a warm wind came along and took the mother's place, blowing a generous pillow right beneath the eaglet. Though wobbling unsteadily, the young one kept stretching his wings out as far as he could. For a moment, he floated gently, lightly. He let out a joyous squawk of excitement. "Eeeeeee! Look at me, I'm flying!"

The great boulder prepared for contact, reaching unseen out toward the young eagle as if with open arms. But then, the eaglet looked down toward him again. He forgot all too quickly. Frantically, the young wings flapped up and down, again fighting the friendly wind. The eaglet's body angled abruptly toward the boulder. If only the boulder could soften his landing!

Beating the air with desperate strokes, the eaglet tried to grab at its granite with his claws, then tried to lower the front edge of his awkwardly large wings—anything to slow himself. He skidded across the entire breadth of the rock, burning long and hard on his belly toward its far end. All three eagles felt their chests pounding as he slid toward the possibility of further injury, even death. It was a steep drop to the next ledge.

He came to a stop just at the boulder's edge so abruptly it seemed as if an invisible wall had come up to stop him. The boulder had done what he could within his limitations.

The mother eagle circled lower, trying to surmise the condition of her young, who lay sprawled and dazed, wings hanging over the boulder's sides. She chose not to come to his aid but hovered nearby, calling encouragement. Finally, after endless quiet moments, she saw him pull his legs in awkwardly beneath himself and push up to a wobbly stance, shaking his feathers.

Relieved, she started back toward her mate. Just then, the whole mountain began to quiver. The rumbling grew louder, ever closer. The mountain mother shuddered; the boulder shook; the eaglet tensed. For a fleeting moment of confusion, they both blamed the unfamiliar only on each other.

The great mountain mother, though she trembled more and more, was locked into her own passivity. Through the centuries, she had been formed. Through aeons, she'd remained. Surrounded by so many she had helped to grow and to flourish, she recognized little else than her own immortality. Secure in her vastness, she simply stood in her place, fulfilling her purpose. Always it had been. Always, surely, it would be.

Only the eagles knew they must act. Satisfied that his offspring had landed without injury, the tiercel forced himself to jet away from the boulder toward the mountain's highest peaks, calling out to his mate to join him, "Eeeeeeaa! Come, come, for now we must let our brazen baby take care of himself! There may be a greater threat to us all drawing near..."

Reluctantly heeding his call, the hen angled sharply without hesitation to soar with her mate. Together, they circled above the mountain, exchanging throaty signals as they scrutinized everything within range of their keen vision. They were all too aware that this world of craggy nesting nooks and verdant slopes, which yawned beneath them each new day to pop up tasty gophers and rabbits, was there for their need and their pleasure only for the day.

They knew, as well, that endings must come before new beginnings. Though they'd discovered nothing yet, their innermost senses warned them that change was approaching—big change affecting the entire world as they and their ancestors had known it.

The sun was still high when they allowed their sense of foreboding to split the air between them. Looking back toward each other only once, they moved resolutely in opposite directions—he, off on a long flight toward discovery to identify the threat to the territory their ancestors had claimed for them many generations ago and to defeat it, if necessary—even if it meant a battle unto death.

Calling out a final "Eeeeooww," the female turned from her mate and zoomed toward a solitary hunt. Their foolish young adventurer would need his nourishment more than ever. He would not be so ready to take on the world yet, away from the security of their nest. His bold foray had introduced him to fear. Now he must learn to overcome it. She would help him.

Far beneath her, a foolish ball of gray fur bolted from one scrub bush to another. Soundlessly, the mother eagle zoomed down, an arrow shot from nature's bow. She plucked the poor mouse out of the hole it was trying to enter just before its tail disappeared.

Heading back toward her young, she found him shivering on the boulder. With new respect, his eyes followed her easy descent through the brilliant blue, a gray lump of fur dangling from her talons. Dropping the rodent at his feet, she floated down right beside him.

Pouncing on cue, he squeezed his own talons around the still-warm body of the unfortunate mouse and killed it again in rehearsed ritual. This he knew well how to do. Watching him tear quite skillfully through the fur into the flesh with his beak, his mother resisted the urge to fly off again. This was not the time for her son to practice survival on his own in the world of dirt and rock and bush. She and her mate would hunt together some other ordinary day. This day, she remained on the boulder next to the eaglet and watched the skies for his father's winged shadow.

2

By midmorning, heavy swirls of dust and noise traveled the winds. Vibrations shimmied across the valley floor to the mountain mother, played mischievously around her base, and ran tickling up her sides to the top, like a thumb rippling across piano keys. Pores of awareness long asleep deep within the large boulder finally began to open. What was this unfamiliar trembling, this shaking, reaching into his very core? The baby eagle sidled closer to his mother. Both birds dug deeper into the boulder's granite with their needle-like claws. The boulder didn't mind. His awareness was shared. He found solace in that, and in being there for them—as he was meant to be.

Far across the valley, the tiercel settled onto a rock ledge, hoping for a brief rest. But even the ledge shook nervously beneath him. Pebbles tumbled past him. He cocked his white head from side to side, neck feathers ruffled. The steady beating in his chest grew harder, faster, louder, demanding to know. What was this mysterious energy? What threat of change did it carry? He had met many challenges and conquered them, some more easily than others, but, always, first, he had learned to understand. Only where there was lack of knowledge lurked the ominous threat of defeat.

His weariness subsided. He would not approach the challenge with fear. Pushing off from the ledge, he opened his mighty wings to maximum spread and rocketed upward, then leveled off high above to examine the valley with practiced eye. Straight toward the heart of confusion, he flew onward. His whole world was abristle. Tempting morsels darted wildly, brazenly out in the open, oblivious to his menacing shadow. But for once, this predator's eye was focused only to feed his brain. Ignoring his instincts, as well as his crop, he marked a straight line through the air, searching for the source of disturbance.

As he neared the valley's northeast opening between the sprawling foothills, his black eyes telescoped toward unusual movement below. Narrowing his wing span, the eagle aimed lower and adjusted his feathers to slow his speed. There, just below him now, was a creature like none he had ever seen or heard or felt, a mammoth serpent crackling with purpose and coughing up huge clouds of dust, as it slithered over the outer lip of the valley's bowl. It was a disjointed beast with many yellow eyes and sharp beaks, legs that rolled, and tall necks leading an assault against the valley, raising and lowering stiffly as the beast lurched forward, loudly belching black smoke. Everything that could darted from its path. The monster crumpled all else, even once-proud grasses, into groveling slime beneath its relentless charge.

It had no discernible wings, made no attempt to take to the skies that the eagle's father had marked before him long ago. Still, the giant bird sensed a threat not only to his own, but to the mountain, the entire valley, and all those for whom many ordinary days had opened and closed there. Somehow, the eagle understood that nothing would ever be the same. He must at least try to do something to stop it! He had killed serpents, eaten them, fed them to his young. But none like this...

Nevertheless. He steeled himself, readied his talons, closed wings tight to the body, and dove, a sleek black-and-white torpedo aimed straight for its mark. Silently, swiftly he plummeted. He would pierce its head, strike at its yellow eyes, squeeze the life from its shimmering bellies. Closer. Closer.

It was only at the last moment, just before contact, that the eagle's reflection glared back at him from the shiny gray shell, and he perceived its hardness. Turning with lightning speed, he thrust his legs out and screeched across the beast's back, leaving only long, deep scratches along its surface.

"Get a load o' that eagle!" the beast cried out. "He just dive-bombed us!"

Quickly, the eagle surmised the futility of his efforts. Checking his course, he sailed to the right back toward the nest. He must gather his family, whisk them away without delay on to a new beginning away from the beast and its charge of change.

But too late! He had stirred its anger! A short, round hairy figure reached for a brown stick and pointed it toward the retreating bird.

"No!" cried another part of the beast, slapping out to dislodge the stick.

Ceerraackk! A strangely echoing pop was the last sound the tiercel heard before he started careening toward the ground, suddenly out of control. He did not hear the thud of his body. Nor the loud smack of a man's fist against the jaw of his killer.

3

"Whatsa matter wit you, you got no respect? You shoot livin' tings right outa the air? That was the eagle, man! You don' even care 'bout the freedom you got? That eagle, he stan' for the freedom! You kill your own freedom? What I run away from my homeland and barely make it across the sea to find?"

Santos Martinez rubbed the back of his big hand, glaring down at Willie with moist dark eyes. Willie's freckled arms looked shorter and fatter as he snatched futilely at the rusted metal sides of the truck, trying to pull himself back up from the corner of its bed. His shock turned to rage when he finally had to give in and turn over into a crawl like a baby to push himself back up on to his feet. Face beet-red, he charged like a bull toward the taller man, fists raised.

"What gives you the right to come sneakin' over here in a rickety boat and think you can just grab the freedom what my great granddaddy fought for? My cousin even died for it not too long ago! You think you can tell me how I should treat what's my hard-earned natural-born heritage? What about us humans? Didn't you see it, Mr. Tender Heart? That crazy bird attacked us!"

"All right, that's enough, you two. Break it up!" hollered Jake, pushing both his arms in between the two men's chests and shoving them apart. Everyone had stopped working. Each leaning on whatever tool he'd been using when the eagle had first startled them all, they'd grabbed the precious moment of rest, watching the foray unfold.

"Jake, you know you didn't need to shoot that eagle. That was a downright *mean* thing to do. There oughta be a law against shootin' eagles. Santos, same goes for you whallopin' on Jake. You need to tame that Cuban temper of yours. Heed my warning. You'll both be gone after the next trip to town if you can't get along. Plenty more waitin' for work back there."

Both men shot looks of quiet contempt toward the other as they moved to opposite sides of the truck.

"Now, we got important work here." Jake continued, "Let's get back to it."

"But what about the eagle? We not gonna go fin' it, maybe help it?"

"Man, you know as well as I do there's no savin' that eagle," said Jake matter-of-factly. "That was a clean shot, and that there's a dead bird, else we *would* try to help it. My guess is it's beyond help, Santos. And we've still got a job to do." He raised his voice to a commanding shout, "Back to work, you lazy slackers! Don't lean on those shovels! Dig with em!"

Overcome by emotion, Santos had to lean his strongly muscled body against the truck to stay upright. He yearned to jump free of the caravan, track the eagle down, and see if he could still do something for it. Jake didn't know everything. He could only guess like the rest of them. Maybe there was still time to do something. Maybe the big bird was just nipped enough to get knocked out of the sky. Maybe it landed on something soft. Maybe he could still help it! None of them had any idea what it was like to want to fly so bad and have others take away your wings!

But like the others, Santos was on the clock. The vertebrae of the snake, after all, was only made up of men and machines, its cartilage, their common goals. Men needed roads, and that's what they were here to lay behind them. They, too, were a part of the day, the sweat on their muscled backs glistening from the same raging fire as did the oil of the bald eagle's feathers. They were doing their jobs, killing for food, building for their families.

With heavy chest, Santos snagged a pick and leaped over the side of the truck. Down deep in his heavy heart, he felt sure the eagle had to be dead. What could he do for it now anyway other than give it a decent burial? He hoisted the pick over his head and swung it into the ground, thrusting his anger into the hard earth. Eventually, he found the rhythm again and made his way forward with the others, crescendo in unison, step-by-step, wheel by wheel, front loader, backhoe, shovel and pick, boots on the ground.

Willie could stand it only so long. He stopped to wipe his ruddy forehead with the back of his arm and couldn't help sneering at Santos, "It's only a dumb bird, you ignorant immigrant! Didn't you ever go huntin' with your Pa in Cuba? You a mama's boy, or somethin'?"

Santos dropped the pick right in his tracks and took two long steps toward him, his 6'2" frame quickly dwarfing Willie.

"That was not just any bird, Willie! That was the eagle, you blind American redneck! You too blind to know the diffrance? You wan' dumb? Look in the mirror! You would be lucky havin' brains like your eagle!" Santos yelled down into his face, clenching his fists again, daring him to respond.

"I said that's enough!" the foreman warned. "Santos, go to the front on the other side. Willie, bring up the rear! This is your last chance to stay on this line!"

Jake scolded, they obeyed, as if he were the teacher, and they the hotheaded boys in school. Of course, Santos was painfully aware of his childishness. He'd surprised himself with his uncontrolled explosion of anger. He funneled it toward the hard ground for the rest of the day, apart from the others and at odds, driven by a separate fury, though they all moved forward together according to their joined purpose.

Finally, the hot sun began its descent toward the horizon, and the trucks circled to set up camp. A cooling breeze tickled the back of Santos' neck. He knew he had to get away by himself to deal with the anger and the shame, to allow this deep sadness to come to the top, see it, hold it, fully express it so he wouldn't boil over again.

Shouting over his shoulder to anyone who might hear, "I'm goin' for a walk," he aimed directly into the blackening mouth of the woods by the trail. They'd only progressed a few miles from where the eagle had fallen. His body screamed for rest, but he had to see if he could find it. He shuddered, visualizing the once-great bird crashing helplessly through the pines along the west rim of the valley as if it were happening again and again.

His long legs took big strides, hurrying to get him there and back before the dark had completely enveloped him. By now, the sun was a bright-orange ball, burning its way down behind the trees. Santos squinted, his eyes watering as he searched for the pine with one high branch broken at a sharp angle.

"Dammit, Willie!" he cursed under his breath, shoving his hands deep into his pockets. "You are more than dumb! You are heartless! Why you got no grateful heart? Why you murder this very great symbol for freedom, an' you not even think about it?"

Renewed rage catapulted him into a full run. Blinded by a sudden torrent of shameless tears, he galloped through the woods, oblivious to his surroundings. Finally out of breath, he plopped thankfully onto a birch trunk that stretched for him across the path, probably also a once-proud soldier struck down by lightning, now slowly dying. Santos forced big gulps of air down into his lungs past the pain, then struggled up again, resuming a slow walk.

His eyes were cast downward, watching his feet work through the grass, when a flurry of sound startled him to a halt. He looked up just in time to see a winged shadow burst from the ground and shoot skyward to the north, directly away from a tall pine. There it was—a broken branch near the top, dangling at a sharp angle. Santos froze in his tracks, hair prickling on the back of his neck. That was the tree the eagle had crashed through! The eagle was alive still!

Or had Santos just witnessed an eagle's spirit rising? The culture of his youth was rife with belief in such spirits. "Only superstitions," Santos had always scoffed for all to hear. Now he caught himself wondering—had they known something he had not?

Shivering, he moved warily toward the spot where he'd seen the bird lift off. Twigs snapped like popcorn under his feet.

One minute, the air was dancing with the lively scent of pine—then it was just hanging there, so heavy with the stench of death, his nostrils burned. He looked down again and saw it there in the middle of the forest floor, about eight feet from the pine's base, a once-proud and graceful eagle sprawled in a wet feathered heap, flies buzzing all around it in noisy, pesky disrespect.

"Carramba!" Santos whistled. Less than a foot from its beak was an equally lifeless jackrabbit.

Santos held his breath and jumped toward the open, away from the trees, hoping to clear his mind as well as his senses. For only a second, he was tempted to suspect that Esperanza, the old *brujerio* he and his young friends had always laughed about, had followed him across the sea to prove her magic powers to him after all, perhaps to punish him for deserting his motherland!

One thing was for sure—the big bird that had scraped their front loader that afternoon hadn't been carrying anything. Santos could still see the eagle in all its fury, wings arched close to its body, scraping empty talons across the gray metal with furious courage.

Questions swirling around in his mind, he stretched up as tall as he could and scanned the nearby treetops. His eyes caught her movement just as she shifted position. There it was, barely discernible through the foliage of a cottonwood branch about thirty yards away, a dark, brooding shape.

Santos stiffened, trying to ignore the chill moving up his spine. A ghost? He backed away, forcing his eyes again to the awful scene on the ground. The dead eagle was still there. So was the dead rabbit. Strange, but not impossible. Santos struggled to steer his mind between moguls of emotion.

Think! Think, Santos! Be still, and just think. Half-afraid he wouldn't see anything at all this time, he aimed his gaze again toward the tree with the broken branch.

"That is a real eagle up there!" he announced aloud to Esperanza, just in case she was listening, as much as to his own gullible brain. "I think it is even bigger than the unfortunate one on the ground."

The eagle turned its head and seemed to return his gaze. He'd been too loud. He sucked in a deep breath, trying not to move, afraid he'd already scared it away. But the eagle in the tree seemed determined to outwait him. It turned its head back away from him to look straight ahead.

Was it his imagination, or did this eagle seem stooped, not typically proud-looking but bent a bit, as if in a posture of sadness? One thing was becoming obvious, this eagle was no stranger to the other. It looked so lonely! Had they been mates? Santos waited for what seemed like hours, hardly breathing, hoping the eagle in the tree would realize he was no threat and show him whatever it was doing before he'd interrupted with his untimely arrival.

Time moves slowly with no ticking clock, no noise except the wind in the trees to measure it by. The forest opened its black mouth wider, threatening to swallow him whole. He stood his ground. Nothing happened. Finally, moving slowly with what he hoped the eagle would recognize as deep respect, Santos started backing up in the general direction of camp. He didn't want to miss whatever was going to happen next. But now he knew he had to leave before it could.

He'd barely edged away when a lonely stretch of wings sailed across the crimson sky slowly, in mournful procession, down from the broken pine toward the forest floor. Whether the jackrabbit had been like his grandmother's chicken soup, a devoted offer to cure anything, or a testament of love and bereavement like a spray of red roses, Santos was convinced that this was, indeed, the mate of the ill-fated eagle. More than likely, the attack against the caravan had been in this one's protection—Jake was probably right, there must be a nest of eaglets nearby. That would be logical—this was eagle territory. To them, they were not just men and machines building a road—they were invaders destroying their perfect world.

The grief in his chest tightened even more. Was this his way of repaying God's messenger that had awakened him at sunrise on the island, hovering over him as he'd lain there, exhausted, on the rocky shore that early morning, now almost two years ago? He'd rubbed his burning eyes in disbelief at first, then rolled onto his knees on the coarse sand to offer his thanks, "Ay, it is true, finally, I am free! I know now I will soon touch the softer sands of America and be welcomed—a political refugee seeking freedom! Thank you for sending the eagle to tell me it is so, it will be, and for making it so!"

He'd seen many eagles after that during those three long days as he'd waited anxiously for the final portion of his journey. They had helped him forget his fear as he'd watched them from behind a bush, marveling at their intelligence, their strength, their uncanny likeness to humans in so many behaviors. Now he'd even been given the sad privilege of witnessing the remarkable depth of their relationships.

The sun dipped low against the horizon. Santos turned around and started jogging, thinking how much better off people would be if they would try to emulate the big bird instead of shooting at it. He ran faster. He did not want to be lost in the darkness in a strange world again.

4

Sleep melted his rigid body as soon as he hit the cot. In the middle of the night, he suddenly realized he was staring into the darkness and wondered if he'd been asleep at all, and if so, for how long. Had he been dreaming a minute ago, or was he dreaming now? He sat up, feet flat on the cold tent floor, trying to get his bearings.

Only a minute ago, he'd been crouched under the hull of a creaking boat that he knew was barely seaworthy, holding his breath as much as he could so he wouldn't have to smell the fishnet that blanketed him. Then he was leaning over the side, gazing into Marcella's almond-shaped, copper-colored eyes, at the vision of her face floating like a giant sun goddess across the dark green waves. He couldn't seem to figure out if her cheeks were wet from the sea or still streamed with the tears he'd kissed away that last time together before he'd leaped from her, alone and afraid, on to the deck of the boat that was waiting in the wet blackness.

His resolve had never wavered, not until that moment once they'd all decided together—he and Mama' and Papa' and Marcella. But, that night, he'd tried to pull her so close he'd be able to take her with him, right then, her body and spirit completely dissolved into his. Failing that, he'd blurted into the softness of her neck, "Beg me not to go, Marcella! Only ask, and I will not go! Somehow we will find happiness here, as long as we are together!"

For a moment, he'd thought she had weakened too as her arms had tightened around him, and she'd reached up to kiss him again. His broad hands had clasped the thickness of her long black hair, and he'd decided he would never let go. Then she'd pushed against him with the strength they'd both needed. Only her arms had betrayed her feelings, stretching out toward him after she'd pushed him away as if all her fingers were magnets, and she was trying to pull him back. A single strand of her hair had caught on the button of his sleeve, and she'd winced. He would have used it as an excuse to go back and comfort her, but the boat had been shoved away from the shore by the force of his leap, even as one foot was still in the air. Suddenly, he knew he couldn't bear to lose that one tangible piece of Marcella's being. Digging the handkerchief Mama' had made sure he had before he'd left home out of his pocket, he'd lovingly folded it around the strand of hair. He'd known he should duck out of sight right away, but he'd had to glue his eyes onto her shadow until the growing distance between them completely replaced it with a dark void. Only then had he taken a big breath of air and dived into the smelly veil of fishnet.

He'd been kissing the air when he woke in the middle of the night. He held his breath feeling stupid, grateful for once that Joe continued to snore as loudly as ever. Finally convinced it was safe, Santos got up and went out to look at the stars to seek the same solace they'd given him on the island, where he had waited in hiding for the smaller boat to carry him the rest of the way to America. He wondered now as he'd wondered then, did Marcella see the Big Dipper too—was she looking at it now just as he was? And did she see the lion of courage, the bull of strength? Did she marvel tonight, like he, at the massive expanse of the universe that still connected them and try to ask God where He was and why He didn't help them more?

Down deep he knew, and he was sure Marcella and Mama' and Papa' would have no doubt, they'd already been helped more than he'd ever dared hope. Here he was, safe in America, as they'd been promised. So many had tried but had either capsized and drowned, or died of starvation or dehydration, or worse, at the hands of Castro's guards…or languished for years, even now, in filthy prisons.

Why he, Santos, had actually made it across the big ocean, he could only believe was that he was meant to fulfill a special destiny all his own, ordained by God Himself.

He knew, at least, that he would never have to go to the university for artists, his creativity exploited "for the people." He would never have to paint, or carve, or draw for the glory of Castro. He could share with others what was truly in his heart.

"Here you stand, just a boy. But you have more talent than many men," Mama' had marveled aloud, glowing as she'd hugged the picture her twelve-year-old son had drawn of her as a birthday gift tight against her big bosom. "When you have such talent at so young an age, you must hold it close to your heart just like this with great respect."

She'd smiled broadly at him, patting his cheek, holding his artwork out for him to see as if he hadn't yet. "Yes, this is such a beautiful gift from a son to his mother. But it is also a gift...to you." Her shining eyes had gazed up at the dingy ceiling of their little house as if it had been blue sky with golden angels dancing around on puffy clouds. "We must both cherish our gift."

They had all fallen into nervous silence as soon as she'd uttered the words. Someone could always be listening. Castro wanted to be their God now.

That sweet day seemed so long ago, but it was still as fresh to Santos as if it had happened yesterday. Perhaps someday he would paint just some of the stars he saw now onto a piece of black velvet—if, indeed, it would ever be possible to recreate such beauty. He would frame it in gold filigree and give it to Mama'.

God willing, I get that chance, he thought. Cupping the small key and chain in his pocket, he offered thanks and asked for protection for Mama' and Papa' and Marcella, still waiting at home—most of all, he prayed they would suffer no retaliation for his escape—that his last letters had reached them, and he could figure out a way to get them here safely, and soon.

For now, he had to go back into the lean-to, fold his tired body up on the cot that was too short for his lanky frame, and at least get some rest, if not sleep. Tomorrow would be a hard day. He had never plowed through a mountain before. But they were getting closer. He closed his eyes, trying to shut out the feeling of dread that sat like a rock on his chest.

5

Across the valley, while Santos and Willie and all the men still slept, the eaglet stirred with hunger. Dawn brushed the sky with bold strokes of pale pink. The young bird raised his head again, but no dark speck grew bigger, closer, carrying food for his belly. He stepped warily over twigs and leaves, hoping again to feel the lift that had found him so easily in the nest, when he'd first barely opened his wings. It was so effortless in the beginning, as if something had blown him upward from beneath and held him aloft.

Yesterday, after many strange moments of aloneness, he had bravely pushed himself away from the boulder toward the late-afternoon sky to follow the course of his father and mother and find them. He'd only managed to clear the straggly bushes on the ledge just beneath them— barely. Thrashing ever lower, he'd tumbled back down again and again into their midst. Exhausted, he'd finally pulled himself in as close as he could, trying to shut out the cold dampness, and settled in for the night where he was.

Now, as the sun cast a beckoning shaft of golden sparkle across the familiar boulder, the eaglet aimed his gaze toward it as he had in the nest. With each foray, surely, his flight would become more certain, his wings more steady, his back more strong. At the moment, he just wanted to make it to the boulder and wait there until his father and mother returned and everything was once again as it was, and should be. His crop would be filled, and he would soon grow to soar like them and catch his own prey.

Perhaps he truly sensed as he lifted off that his mother drew near, beating the air with doleful determination. Her watchful eyes caught his awkward flight. Her young was safe and gaining strength, but for now she was still needed. Wearily, she turned toward the stream of water, searching for an easy catch.

The man was standing right there by the water's edge. Though her heart was impatient, she hovered close, keenly aware of his every move. There was something shiny in his hand. He was eyeing the meal that was meant for her, three streaks of silver shimmering near the water's surface. Wings poised in hushed attention, she hung cautiously, still high above.

Santos flipped the bucket upside down again to make sure all the water dripped out. Everybody in camp was full and satisfied. He had learned only too well on meager rations that nature demanded back all that wasn't needed. Turning back toward camp, he took a deep, grateful breath of the whole morning, invigorated by the fresh air. The brisk scent of sage woke all his senses; he could hear a cacophony of sounds, crickets, mockingbirds, bullfrogs, shouting, "Good morning!" The sun glowed rosy on the mountain. It would be so easy just to immerse himself in the wonder and the task of the day, to ignore the aching within. He had always marveled at the beauty around him with tremendous gratitude, felt its impact more deeply than others seemed to. He pitied them for what they were missing. If only he could capture on canvas the brilliant mosaic spun before all of humanity each and every day, help everyone else see what he saw, all the layers from God's palette just as it existed, there for the taking. If only he could, and they would.

"Please do not think me too proud or loco," he'd announced to Mama' and Papa' that afternoon just before supper. They'd both turned away from their tasks, as they always had when Santos had something important to say. He could still see them: Papa' peering in through the screen from the back porch, where he'd been trying to scrub his rough hands clean of tobacco stains, and Mama', sneaking an approving sniff of the rare and precious lobster claw stew she'd just stirred before replacing the lid and turning to look him in the eye, wiping her short but deft fingers on her apron.

"I believe…God wants me to…to help others see the beauty all around them with my art!" he'd stammered.

His father had grinned with obvious tolerance, nodding his head as he'd resumed his scrubbing. "Si, si! It is good, you paint this world with your rosy eyes, maybe others see what you see! Bueno! We need more rosy eyes in this world, fewer green worms spitting the juice of the plant."

"He speaks of his gift, Manuel, the gift bestowed upon him by God Himself!" Mama' had shouted to her husband on the porch. Then she'd clasped her hand over her mouth, hoping there were no soldiers within earshot.

Encouraged by her defense, Santos had continued, his voice hushed but firm, "Yes, and God has given me this gift to use. He speaks to me, I know he does, through this need that wells up from my soul!"

"Si, si, and when God speaks, a good son listens!" Her hands had flown in a declaration of authority to her thick waist, as Papa's head shook back and forth, now resolute with tolerance.

Santos had known that neither expected what he must now say. Both to assure he wouldn't stop, and that they both had heard and understood, he'd blurted out the next sentence, "I must be free to paint for God, not for Castro!"

Instinctively, they'd all gone rigid, their bodies frozen with the fear in their hearts that was always there, as pent-up feelings rushed up and out across the tongue and into the possible earshot of someone who might report them. It was such a blatant declaration. They had heard too many times how the sin of individuality had been punished severely through prison, or torture, or worse.

Recalling his words now, Santos stiffened. He had little to show for his boldness then. Since arriving in America, his only artistic achievement was to destroy that which was in order to help control what would be. Survival seemed to dictate that he had no choice, at least for now. Sometimes, he let himself wonder, why didn't God help him if He wanted him to paint so much? But, then, he remembered his gratitude, his safe arrival here in America, and finding this job to pay his way, each time praying the little he could sneak home through his contact would get to them and not be seized by Castro's guard, that the little bit more he was able to save would grow into a rescue fund for them all soon. The time for his art would come in God's good time. Still, he couldn't help wondering, was this what he was meant to do? The answer came: *At least, for now.*

And so, once again on that fateful morning, he turned his strong, tanned body back toward camp with a new resolve. He'd taken only a few steps when a strange noise whistled behind him. His body went rigid. He whirled around, fearing the sting of a snake. Instead, he watched in stunned relief as a huge bald eagle glazed the water with ready talons and plucked with ease one of his cast-off trout, still wriggling near the surface. Like a graceful skater on ice, the eagle skimmed across without hesitation, then climbed at an easy angle back toward the clouds.

Santos watched the eagle's flight in awe. Somehow, he knew that this was the mate once again. Their paths seemed destined to cross. He followed its trek as far as he could, consumed with admiration, until it descended with obvious purpose toward the mountain's base, out of his vision.

Toward the mountain! Reality slammed into Santos. His arms and legs felt weighted down with a thousand pounds, as he tried to run like lightning back to camp, shouting, "The mountain! We cannot dynamite the mountain!"

Things were becoming crucial now. It was only a matter of days! They were nearly finished packing, about to roll out, when he reached them, breathless. Santos pulled himself up straight and blurted between deep breaths, "More days, more time…the eagles, they need more time! We have to wait. We cannot hit the mountain yet. It is their home!"

Every man stopped moving. Keeping his head bent over the map he'd been studying, Jake raised only his eyes quizzically toward Santos.

"You got some sort of problem with the job all of a sudden, now that we've made it all this way?" he asked through clenched teeth, his patience with "the Cuban" showing obvious signs of wearing thin.

Boldly, Santos strode two steps closer. "It is the eagle widow, sir! She has babies, I know! Straight toward the mountain, she flew just now, and she carry the fish I just threw back in. You should have seen her scoop it right up!"

Jake folded the map with exaggerated purpose. Everyone else remained frozen, speechless. Santos stood at surprised attention, tensed and ready to spring at the first snicker. No one dared.

"I'm real sorry to hear that," Jake announced drolly, accentuating every syllable. He strolled with exaggerated calm toward the truck, twisting into a tight roll the already-folded map. "But I have a feeling they won't hang around long, Santos. They'll probably decide to migrate out of here before any more of 'em gets hurt."

"What if they cannot yet fly?" cried Santos, hot on his heels. "We just gonna let 'em die?"

He trailed Jake all the way to the truck and saw him place the map of the mountain and their road to it, through it, and on beyond next to the driver's seat. There would be no turning back. Men had staked their claim with the stroke of a pen, and now they were here to take it. Eagles, hawks, deer and mice, anything in the way, beware! With a cold chill, Santos came to full realization.

"It is possible we can move them, all of us, before we blow up the mountain!" he persisted, following inches behind Jake all the way around the truck and back toward the tent. "We owe it to the baby eagles after what happened to their papa! Or mama, maybe, I am not sure which is left, but probably the male came after us trying to protect his family!" He shot a look toward Willie, daring him to react, amazed at his own boldness, but keeping his jaw set. The men began to mill around, a few of them shaking their heads.

"Look, Santos, I appreciate where you're comin' from, really, I do. I got nothin' against eagles or any kind of bird. And you're right, eagles are pretty special to us Americans. Kind of ironic…that probably *was* the daddy bird tryin' to protect his nest. He was fightin' for his family's freedom, even though he stands for ours. And he went and got hisself killed for it. Just like a lotta our soldiers."

"Right!" shouted Santos, encouraged by Jake's admissions. "I mean…but, that's not right, no?"

"Naw, it's not right. You've got a point. I'm not as hard-hearted as I might seem, Santos. Problem is, even if we didn't have a contract to worry about, we have to get this road laid before winter storms move in."

"But I know if we try…"

"The ruckus usually stirs 'em up and rousts 'em out anyway, Santos, don't worry. Those eagles can take care of themselves. And we're workin' against a deadline."

"But we can't—"

"What, are you worried so much about the birds, you don't care about us humans? How about your girl back home, Santos, your ma and pa? You'd better go get your stuff together if you still want to send money home to Cuba and bring 'em all here."

Santos dug his hands deep into his pockets, cupping the post-office key in his fingers. With the other hand, he clutched Marcella's worn letter. Jake had finally gotten to him. He headed toward his cot. All he could hope for now was that the eagles were nesting on the far side of the mountain, away from the blasts that would start in a few days, once the road to its base was completed.

6

His mind raced throughout the night as he tossed and turned on the skinny cot, wondering how many eagles they'd be blasting away from their home. Would they be killing any? What about the babies, were they mature enough to make it out of the nest? A hot cone of morning sunlight finally forced his eyes open; he got up groggily, rolled up his bedding, and slouched with it toward the waiting trucks. Visions of eagles in large groups milling about along the island stream played as vividly in his mind's eye as when he had watched them with such admiration just a few years ago.

The fishing boat had creaked to the island's edge hours before dawn. He shuddered, remembering how they'd had to wade through black, icy water, hip deep, tangled in slimy seaweed. He'd prayed all the way up to the beach that nothing ominous was lurking below, where he couldn't see it, waiting to strike and take him down. Heaving, breathless, he'd sank onto the cold sand, uttering prayers again and again, though his stomach still heaved with nausea.

"Hurry! Get up into the bushes, out of sight! Get under cover! Come on, you've got to get up!" someone warned. With great effort, Santos had dragged himself, crawling up and beneath a stand of bushes, heeding the warning of those more experienced at escaping from the homeland. He could still feel the desperate surge of panic that had washed over him as the tiny, insignificant shadow of the fishing boat that had so steadfastly carried them thus far disappeared back into the open mouth of the sea. Suddenly they were left there, alone and hungry, exhausted and sick, afraid of what might be lying in wait just an inch away in the dark, but knowing eventually they would have to move if they were to survive at all. They could only wait, and hope, and pray, until the next boat came for them, as they'd been promised.

The eagle had scared him half out of his wits at first. Despite the shivering that wouldn't be quelled in the night, Santos had finally given in to sleep, or passed out, he wasn't sure which. All he knew was that he'd been startled awake by a cold, fast wind moving over him. With wide eyes, he'd watched the imposing figure sweep toward the first golden brush of dawn. Had he died? Was he still asleep? Was this a nightmare, or a dream? Was he already in America? Was this Freedom itself come to welcome him?

Freedom! He still remembered sitting bolt upright, suddenly realizing he was going to make it. He was on his way to freedom, and God had sent the eagle to assure him. Wasn't the eagle the very symbol of the free world, of America? Soon, Santos knew he would be free to be himself, away from the relentless control and manipulation he had struggled against in Cuba. He'd always felt that he was meant to be, to do so much more than the great leader had allowed. His faith had never wavered. Now God had sent him a sign. It was all meant to be, just as he and Mama' and Papa' and Marcella had always believed.

After that, the waiting had been more bearable. It almost seemed the Americans had arranged a welcoming site, with the island hosted by so many of the black-and-white winged giants. Even the young eagles that had not yet earned their white heads exuded majesty, power, and freedom. Santos had watched in fascination from his hiding place, as throngs of eagles young and old had rested together in common spirit and mutual respect, pruning each other, digging with their beaks for mites each in turn, in the ruffled feathers of each others' white necks. He'd marveled at the camaraderie and cooperation they enjoyed together, despite their fierce power. One moment, they would be sitting securely in the midst of a peaceful crowd. The next, they would streak alone into the sky like bolts of lightning seeking a target for sustenance—or just showing off and flying for the fun of it.

Theirs was a lesson of what freedom would truly mean. Santos took it completely to heart. He would follow the eagles' example and work with zeal, preparing for the time when his own loved ones would join him here, all together in love and support of each other. Of course, they would always love their homeland. Always, they would want to return to Cuba and establish a great island of freedom there as well. Maybe someday, when Castro no longer ruled the island with his fist of iron, people like himself who still longed for freedom could have some influence, help somehow.

One dream at a time. For now, Santos would work hard and save money and hold Marcella close to his heart, not just in it. The day would come when he could send for her and Mama' and Papa'—if it wasn't too late. He blinked the moistness away from his eyes.

"Come on, Santos, you'll miss the train!"

"I'm comin'!" he shouted. Jarred into the present, he steeled himself and hustled out to the truck, jumped up on the rear bumper and over the side. He landed almost on top of Willie, who squinted sideways at him, then surprised him with a faint, apologetic grin. Santos nodded a stiff acknowledgement and leaned against the truck beside him. Willie was the last person he would have expected to reach, but it felt good to see the slightest sign of caring, maybe—even if it was too late to do much good for the eagles now.

7

Wearily, the mother eagle made her way over the last tall clump of pines. Ah, there it was, the long, flat boulder, sparkling in the morning sunlight—such a welcoming friend, calling, as always, "Come, please, rest on me! I don't mind, in fact, I thrive on your company."

For many days, ever since she, herself, had first slid so ungracefully across his back, they had traded energies right there on the side of the mountain, their special place of shared purpose—of mutual significance. Now, eyeing her fledgling, hunched and motionless, almost glued to the security of its granite, which he'd finally managed to get to again, she felt new energies washing away the tiredness in her bones. Warming inside, she eased her grip and allowed the trout to land with a thud right next to him, eager for his reaction. He did not disappoint. He came swiftly to life, attacking, ripping the silver skin of the trout wide open with ravenous hunger.

"Yes, yes, fill your crop, as you have learned. Prepare yourself now, thrive tomorrow. Eat, grow strong, and prepare to learn more." She clucked soft encouragement, hoping he grasped the importance of the lesson, as she struggled to calm the panic within. He would have to learn quickly, grow to be fast and sure enough to chase their prey into the open so she could close in for the kill. Would they ever be able to play together the song of swift precision that seldom missed, as she and his father had played? She could only hope. Alone, the hunt would be difficult.

As soon as his crop was full and she had taken her own turn cleaning every bone of all the red flesh, the mother eagle pushed off from the boulder. Skimming back and forth across the brush, she landed with ease again and again in a nearby clearing, then flew back to the boulder, coaxing her son, "Come, you must put down your fear and make courage your shield, or you will never dart across the skies like your father."

Urged on by the proud vision, the eaglet sprang off the boulder and dove into the ocean of air, his lungs buoyant with hope. But inexperience weighed him down quickly. He began to sink. "Eeeeoww! I'm falling!"

Her wings stretched like open arms, the mother swam underneath and caught the young one on her back. Dazed, he rode there, allowing himself to be carried skyward, up toward the clouds. Had he not fallen before he was ready, his muscles could have been properly matured to lift him without all this work on her part. As it was, her offspring seemed to feel no shame in riding upon his mother's back.

"Eeeeeh!" he squawked. "It's so easy this way! Carry me up, up, up!"

Again, as if on cue, she dropped suddenly out from beneath him and swooped away, leaving him hanging, surprised, but afloat.

"Eeeaaah!" he called out to her. "Look at me, I can fly!"

He flapped his young wings frantically, trying to keep from sinking again. No use! His immature body had not yet learned to trust his wings, nor the willing cushion of air that kept trying to buoy him. "Eeeeeh! Mama, where are you? I need you."

Like magic, she was there again, lifting him from beneath, and he was safe, thrilling to the gentle caress of the wind flowing through his feathers. Again, she dropped away, and he had to sail solo—if only for a very little while. But each time was longer than the time before. He was learning. They would know how much at the time of the next hunt.

Around midday, a foolish rabbit scampered from one bush to another at the far end of their path, perhaps thinking he was faster than they. He did not escape the mother's sharp vision. Angling the lower flap of her wings, she thrust her talons out beneath her to slow her speed. Mustering all his strength just to hold steady enough to follow, the eaglet tensed every muscle, tuned every nerve in to her lead. She pounced. Excitedly, he dropped in behind her. In a flurry of beating wings and dagger-like claws, they managed to make a meal of the hapless creature.

Their hunt had been awkward, far from the grace she had known with her mate. Nevertheless, they had achieved the goal. Perhaps before she weakened too much from her own hunger, he would strengthen and rise up to the billows of white and purple and gold and blue, soaring like his father high above, there to float on a stream of air, waiting to streak like a hunter's bullet toward whatever prey she could rustle from hiding.

Without her mate, the once-natural, pulsating rhythm of life now blared with uncertainty. Once-simple challenges loomed as obstacles, always ahead, in her path. But she knew their proud offspring would not take long to reach the awesome peak of his abilities. She only needed time to help him find his power.

In the meantime, since the glistening boulder seemed to have a magnetic hold on the young eaglet, she too would accept it as home. Content in its familiar role of stalwart protector, the long body of gathered granite collected the sun's heat all day, holding it close within until the daylight began to fade. Only then it would emit its warmth, ever so slowly, as it was meant to do. The two big birds would roost in comfort, their bodies in turn warming the boulder. At times, it almost seemed that everything was as it should be, after all.

But not for long! One crisp morning, the lull of ordinary noises hushed to alert awareness. Again, the whole world began to shake—ground, bushes, leaves, pines, needles, pebbles, boulders large and small. Even the towering mountain trembled nervously. Men and machines were assaulting the peace of her valley.

With quiet courage, the hen eagle managed to subdue the fluttering in her chest and nudged the eaglet all the more firmly toward the day's lessons. First in front and then beside the eaglet, back and forth all morning, she coaxed him on until their bellies were screaming to be filled. But nothing dared show itself. All that breathed had burrowed deep into hiding, hearts drumming.

It wasn't until the sun had reached its highest point that finally, slowly, with ebbs and flows, the rumbling stopped, the coughing, chugging beasts corralled. Eerie stillness replaced the noise, empty of the usual chirps and rustles, calls and answers. The air hung heavy, ominous, seeming almost devoid of life.

The eagles sank to rest on the boulder, hushed and waiting. What had happened? What might happen next? Where would they find sustenance? At long last, the mother eagle angled out into the silence, catching an easy lift on a shaft of air, as a spray of sunlight tickled her feathers in warm flirtation. Everything here felt as it should. Perhaps, now, it would be again.

She could not have known that the valley's reprise was a result only of men, too, needing sustenance. They had stopped once again by the stream, where the water burst forth with thick rushes of trout and salmon. Willie and Santos had not really made peace with each other. Jake had ordered them to go to the stream together and not to come back until they had successfully cast their fly rods into the water side by side, enough time to "catch as much as you can for every single man. And do it as fast as you can, so we can all get back to work as quick as possible, or we'll never get this job we came here to do done on schedule!"

And so it was that as the eagle neared the ribbon of water, she spotted not just one human, but another beside him, as well. She could not have known that this was the very man who had shot her mate. She only knew that he held something silver. Perhaps they were hoping to eat the food that was destined for her and her young!

Santos saw the big bird first. He'd watched her approach from the corner of his eye, admiring the stealth of her landing in a birch tree a couple of feet from the water's edge. Casually, he cast his line in the other direction, hoping Willie wouldn't see her, wondering what he might do if he did. From her perch, she studied them intently, completely motionless, not even seeming to breathe.

"Hey! There's your girlfriend!" Willie crowed, slapping his arm backward against Santos' chest. So intent was his distraction by the imposing bird, and how she was studying their every move, that Santos was almost knocked off balance.

"Look! She's up in that tree!" Willie cried, pointing. There seemed to be honest pleasure in his squeal. Santos looked sideways at him, suspicious.

"Shhh!" he admonished, still watching the eagle. "Do not scare her away! I think maybe she has come for dinner!" He shot a quick glare at Willie. "You will not hurt one feather on this great bird, no?"

Willie's gaze didn't leave the eagle. "Whatcha think, I want the other jaw sore? Naw, don't worry." He couldn't seem to help chuckling drolly, "My gun's back on the truck anyway."

His black eyes fired up, aiming at Willie like daggers, Santos drew all of his six-foot stature up as tall as he could, puffed out his broad chest, and stepped toward the shorter but big-muscled man. Willie edged back, reached up, and removed his hat with a flourish, running his stubby fingers through his thinning red hair, feigning fear.

The eagle rustled its feathers, as if to lift off in apprehension.

Santos lowered his voice to a hoarse whisper. "Shut up, you hear? This is the widow you made! Try to be nice just a minute! Watch her!"

Sadness flickered in Willie's bright blue eyes as he turned them toward the eagle. All three stood like statues, dancing shadows in the swiftly moving water. Impulsively, Santos leaned over and snatched a wriggling trout from the bucket. He flung it into the air as high as he could to catch her attention and still have it land within the banks of the stream. The trout was still fresh, not a leftover this time. It would not be sluggish in its dive to escape. The eagle would have to move fast.

"What the ——!" What are you doin', you crazy bird lover?" snapped Willie, reclaiming his normal air. "That's our dinner! Hank's gonna fry *us* if you don't..."

A swoosh, a rushed hiss behind them, now directly in front of them, startled the words from his mouth. Both men gasped, as the huge eagle skimmed over the water with weightless grace, wings broad, ailerons bent, talons down, streaming like a jet across and then up. The silver trout, not swift enough, wriggled in tow.

"I'll be a monkey's uncle," Willie breathed softly after a stunned silence. "That was slick."

As if to speak further would be an intrusion, the two men leaned into the fragrant air in a trance, each unto his own thoughts.

It was Santos who finally moved first, tossing his line toward the water. "We better get busy, or Jake *will* fry us for dinner!" he teased.

Still seeming dazed, Willie let out a low whistle and cast his line, not even seeming to notice the jab. Wordlessly, both keenly aware of the sweet harmony of their fishing lines whistling and whirring in and out of the water, Willie and Santos refilled the bucket with ease, for everything had long been as it was meant to be in the mountain valley. It was a land of plenty.

As they turned silently together back toward camp, Santos was tempted to share his story—the escape, the relief, the signal from God, the magic and wonder of the place he had named Eagle Island. They'd shared a moment of magic just now. But he didn't trust anyone that much yet.

Photo by Danielle Egan

8

That evening, after the day's work and dinner were done, Santos slipped away before Willie or anyone else noticed. Thankfully, the summer days offered long hours of light. He had to find out how many eagles there were, if there was a nest, or she was on her own, or maybe even with a large group like the one he'd seen on the island. He wasn't sure what he could do once he found out. Nevertheless, it mattered, and so he had to start somewhere.

The mountain had seemed threateningly near as they'd worked toward it, looming over them like an angry god, warning them not to come any closer. He'd been hiking more than an hour before he finally saw an eagle in majestic motion, rising up on a cool draft, then falling away from a pesky hawk toward the valley floor. Memorizing as well as he could the bird's trajectory and where it might have landed, Santos scrambled up over rocks and brush, ignoring his fatigue as he had when they'd first met. He was no eagle expert, but he hoped this was his old friend.

He climbed to a rock ledge where he could look out over the whole valley, trying to see where she'd landed. Suddenly, there they were, right in front of him—so near he could almost reach out and touch the closest one. Startled backward, he had to catch his balance. He braced for an attack, knowing he'd invaded their territory. Instead, both remained calmly perched on a large boulder, long and flat, gleaming in the glow of dusk as late sunrays highlighted its golden flecks. *They look so regal*, thought Santos, *like a king and queen on their throne.*

One eagle inched sideways toward the other, turning its head almost casually toward the brush, though obviously casting its eye intently his way. Santos was amazed by their calm. This had to be the same eagle. She seemed to sense he was not to be feared.

Though the other was a bit smaller, and not as dramatically colored, its head as brown as its body, they were so alike in size that Santos wondered for a moment if he'd been wrong about the widowhood. When a rustle sounded in the bushes not far from their perch, both heads angled toward it, eyes alert in studied attention. But then the squirrel darted across the clearing, allowing a flash of his tail to be seen for no more than a second, and Santos could tell it was the she-eagle who led the charge, pushing away from the rock with sure strength. The other bird locked in behind her, slightly wobbly in its flight. Santos watched in awe. The mother was clearly teaching her young.

She rushed the ground, disappearing into the bushes where the squirrel had scampered. The younger bird fell in after her, almost seeming to land on her back. Santos couldn't really see what was going on, but he winced at the great flurry of feathers and what seemed to be the painful demise of the small creature. He was surprised to see them reemerge a minute later with no catch. They returned to the boulder, she landing like a feather, the young more like a ball. Even so, Santos thought she seemed weary. How many times had they tried to get food without success? With deepening concern, he sat watching them until it was almost dusk.

He didn't know how he could help. But as he turned regretfully away and headed back to camp, his concern turned to resolve. Somehow, he would have to help them get plenty of food, to help the mother eagle keep her strength and the eaglet to gain his. Santos felt his heart beating faster just at the thought. He jumped over every bush and rock in his path, running all the way, a man obsessed. He had to help them both escape to safety, to live the lives they were meant to live as God intended. Santos had long rebelled against a world where innocence is punished, people and creatures casually destroyed and discarded. He would not be a willing participant in such a world. Not in Cuba. Not in America.

Exhausted, he threw himself on the hard cot without washing up, his mind racing. The best he could figure, there were only about five days left before the eagles would have to fly out of there forever. From what he saw today, they'd never make it. The younger bird was far from ready.

He had to do something, help them some way! How? Sleep couldn't settle into his buzzing mind, so he rolled over and stared unseeing into the darkness. He finally got a crazy idea, and no matter what he tried to replace it with, it kept coming back. He was grinning to himself by the time he rolled back onto his stomach, finally allowing the sleep to come. He'd rehearsed the crazy scheme a thousand times. It would never work! For the life of him, he didn't see how it could. But when he did fall into a deep sleep, his lips were still curling up in a slight smile.

9

The next morning, with every cast of his line toward the water, Santos cast his eyes toward the mountain. He could tell Willie was watching for her too, though neither had said it out loud. Their buckets were almost full by the time a dark spot took shape in the distant gray sky. The she-eagle lazily worked her wings up and down, aiming directly toward the familiar pine. Santos braced himself.

Just as she approached overhead, he reached boldly into the bucket, grabbed a trout from the brisk water, and threw it as high as he could into the airway before her. He held his breath. Without hesitation, she swooped upward. As the helpless fish reached the peak of its trajectory, the eagle clamped on to it with swift, practiced talons. Circling widely, she turned back, dipped briefly toward the open-mouthed men as though she were offering a bow of gratitude, and aimed straight toward the mountain, morning's easy catch in tow.

"Yahoo!" shouted Santos. "She got it!"

Willie had been staring in disbelief, mouth gaping wide. Now he whooped out, too, openly rejoicing for the proud bird. "She sure makes it look easy!" he hollered. "Wonder if she gives lessons?"

"Yes, sure she does!" shouted Santos. "I watch her doing just that for long time yesterday. But her baby..." Santos stopped midsentence, whirling around and gleaming at Willie.

"Yes, sure, lessons!" he exclaimed. "You just make my crazy idea come 'round the whole circle! Now you got to help!"

Willie frowned at him, puzzled. "Huh?"

Santos laughed out loud, his chest tightening with excitement. "Yeah, Willie, good for you, you brilliant!" Caught up in the moment, he threw his arm around Willie's shoulder laughing as he pressed him back toward camp.

"You go crazy all of a sudden, man? You sure are actin' like it! What the devil you talkin' about? I was just makin' conversation, that's all, didn't mean for you to take me so serious..."

"You want to help make things turn out okay for the big birds after all, right?" He didn't wait for Willie to answer. "Then you help me help the mama give the baby some lessons, okay? Come on, I tell you how we gonna help. You need to do something. I need to do something. We need to help. Not hurt."

The two men climbed the river bank side by side, Santos talking as fast as he could, Willie now listening intently. His freckled face began to beam. Soon, he was nodding his head as both men, so different in so many ways, allowed an unexpected bond to develop between them.

10

A nd so it began. After breakfast, according to plan, Willie hid the bucket with three dazed leftover trout still flopping around in the water under a batch of spare picks and shovels. He tossed his flannel shirt ceremoniously over one of the handles.

"What was I thinkin' when I brought this?" he growled almost too loudly. "It's hotter 'n blazes out here!"

All morning, as the ball of summer fire rose relentlessly, consuming their energies, the men pushed themselves across the desert brush, spreading hot asphalt behind them, laying a road where there had been only dirt and pebbles and grit and occasional patches of pine, scrub bushes, and wild flowers. With every ten swings of the pick, Santos swept his gaze across the bright sky, searching for a black speck, for graceful wings.

When lunch break finally came, Willie jumped as nonchalantly as possible down off the truck. "Wait up, man, I gotta take a leak," he announced dramatically, ambling toward the trees. Santos braced himself, checking the face of every man as the truck left Willie behind. No one seemed to notice Willie was acting even weirder than usual. Santos hung around, trying to look casually irritated. As soon as all their backs were turned, he grabbed the pail and raced out, gaining on Willie and then sprinting past him, water jostling and spilling over the edges.

They'd have to make it to the mountain and back and somehow conserve enough energy to work through the afternoon shift. Jumping over scrub bushes, stumbling over rocks, the two completely dissimilar figures, one tall and lean, dark-haired and tanned, agile, gazelle-like—the other, struggling to maneuver over the short grass with stubby legs and stocky frame, fair skin reddening quickly under the rays scorching down from the top of the world. The sweat was a natural part of their day, nothing to pay extra mind to.

"Sh-h-h-h." Santos halted without warning, stopping Willie with the back of his hand. "I find them on a big rock just over this rise."

Scrambling up to the ledge, he reached a hand down for Willie. Old animosities dissolved in the moment, as Willie grabbed on and allowed himself to be pulled up. The movement stirred a sudden buzz then an unnatural hush as the strangers' vibrations rippled out across the valley. With awakening awe, Willie crouched beside Santos, taking it all in.

Appearing almost planted on the boulder just above them, the two eagles came to attention, aware of the disturbance but surprisingly not alarmed. Warmed by their trust, Willie had to swallow once more against rising guilt. He saw Santos raise an index finger to his mouth, signaling caution, patience and readiness combined. He watched nervously as his new friend crept along the narrow ledge below the long boulder and disappeared on the other side. Then he forced his fist as quietly as he could into the brisk water in the bucket by his feet. He grabbed onto the wiggling trout and waited, tensed and listening, afraid he might miss the signal. The air hung heavy around him. Every breath he took seemed jarringly loud. Finally it came, a low whistle, barely audible. Silently sucking in a deeper breath, Willie tightened his grip, pulled the unwilling fish from its refuge, and flung it as high as he could with careful aim, hoping it would come back down directly in front of the eagles. Santos *had* to be crazy. How in blue blazes was this gonna work?

But the she-eagle must have been watching, too, like a revved-up jet on an aircraft carrier waiting for her own signal. Only briefly did she wonder why this species chose to share its sustenance with them and why they chose to make a game of it, as if they had watched her with her mate all those many days ago. Did they sense the struggle of the hunt without her mate now? One of the men had seen her mate on the ground. Had he followed her here? What was his purpose? Did he know the cause of her mate's demise?

Whether out of need or a sixth sense of trust, the mighty bird catapulted off her boulder throne, swam up and snagged the silver scales with ready talons, just as it slid down past the younger bird. Arcing upward, she floated on her back, still holding the fish in a death grip.

Willie could barely smother a cheer, his mouth gaping wide open as he watched in disbelief. What a sight! Talk about a fast learner! He let out his breath slowly, hoping she wouldn't land on the boulder with the fish or drop it in front of the eaglet's eager beak, spoiling her youngster before he'd earned it, and before Santos could make his move.

As if on cue, another trout suddenly swam upward on currents of air right in front of the younger bird. Santos had flung it with skilled aim. He could probably play ball as good as that other Cuban, the one that defected and caused such a ruckus.

"Eeeeooow!" called the mother bird. "A meal just for you. Rise up and take it quickly, while you can."

"Go for it," Willie urged in a whisper, snapped back into the moment.

Santos could only watch in dismay as the eaglet hesitated in apparent confusion.

"Eeeee!" urged its mother. "Snatch it, now."

Finally, the younger bird seemed to get the idea and pushed off toward the flying fish. But too late! Again, the eaglet's timing was off. The fish slipped just beyond his grasp and slithered downward. Determined now, the eaglet streaked after it and pounced triumphantly with a thud seconds after it had dive-bombed the earth, as if that had been his intent all along.

The two men shot quick looks at each other and doubled over, both holding their breath to keep from laughing out loud. "Skill will come," Santos declared breathlessly after he'd made his way back around to Willie. "Today was good start. The young one is smarter and stronger now after that exercise. And at least we know they both have sustenance."

They started climbing back down. "This is where I find them before, on this same boulder," Santos declared with apparent admiration, patting the boulder as they lowered themselves past it. "She seem to be what they have claimed for a while, like second home."

The boulder glistened proudly.

"I wonder where…Ay, caramba! Look up there in that big oak tree, see, Willie? That must be the nest, home number one…man, that is huge!"

Willie sucked in his breath again, "What a mansion! Boy, that must have taken some work puttin' that big thing together." His eyes dropped as a sheet of red shame covered his face, magnifying the freckles.

"Guess we know where to find them tomorrow, yes?" exclaimed Santos, having seen the change in Willie's expression.

"Yeah," agreed Willie quickly, obviously thankful. "We'll just have to keep tryin' 'til he catches on. Kid needs to grow up and make it on his own. It's time!"

Santos raised an eyebrow, grinning at the changing man. "Okay! We help the mama raise up the child. Like uncles."

11

The beast had already lit up its eyes and rolled a half mile before they caught up with it.

Trying to sneak on board unnoticed, Santos and Willie grabbed for their tools and jumped back down to resume work, as if they'd never left the scene.

"Did you *kids* have fun?"

They grimaced as Jake came around from the side. Swinging their picks hard into the rock, neither man ventured a response.

"I hope so, because that's all the *fun* you'll be havin' for awhile. Mess duty every meal 'til I say that's enough, unless you want your pay docked a whole day or more. Just test me."

Something blew within Santos, feelings stifled for too many years, saved up for too long to stay quiet now. Brazenly, he slammed his pick to the ground and stormed over to Jake, his temper seething. "Oh yeah?" he challenged.

"What you t'ink this is, boot camp? Maybe chain gang? You t'ink we criminals, or somet'in'?"

"Cool it, Santos," warned Willie.

"No, I won't cool it!" screamed Santos. "I do my work. I catch the meals. I even cook 'em if you want and clean up too. If I am late, you can dock me. But you do *not* control my life after hours. Santos is not on Jake's clock twenty-four hours every day. And if I wanna try to save the eagles from you, that is *my* business."

He whirled around, astonished at himself, but feeling good, really good. Emboldened because he was still standing, he turned back around again, shaking his finger in Jake's face. "In Cuba, I don' have rights. So I escape Cuba. I leave my family, my sweetheart. I come to America, I go to school, I learn the language really good. I study hard, work hard, now I am in line to be the citizen like you. Yes, my heart still belongs to Cuba. It is my homeland. But I am in line for the American citizen, an' I know I have rights I don' have in Cuba. I know you my boss, not slave owner. I show respect. But you not allowed to treat people like the slave, here in America!"

Yanking his pick back out of the ground, he whirled around again and walked back to the line, leaving Jake in a stunned but controlled state of anger behind him. "You not supposed to treat birds like that, either. Especially not eagles. They stan' for the freedom I put my life on the line to come here for!" he shouted over his shoulder.

A nervous laugh rippled through the gang of shocked men. Their heads followed Santos with admiration as he strutted away then turned toward Jake to glare at him one by one, suddenly on the Cuban's side, glistening eyes and upright postures daring Jake to protest. Shooting a defiant look down the line at each of them, the foreman turned on his heel and marched to the back of the last truck, rolling the map tighter and tighter between his fists. Watching him go, everyone seemed to stand even a little bit taller. When they did turn back to their jobs, it was with a new energy, a fresh sense of importance.

For the rest of the day, Jake seemed to make himself scarce on purpose. Santos was glad, because even though it had felt good to unload with such righteous indignation, he'd never reared up in the face of authority like that. Jake had always treated him right before this had come up. The proud Cuban had to admit he wouldn't want to be in the foreman's place right now. A smidgen of regret pushed against his pride. Maybe he'd apologize next time they came face-to-face. He knew he owed Jake a big debt of gratitude, giving this still-green immigrant a decent-paying job.

But Santos was more sure than ever he was meant to be here for now—if not for his own survival, for the eagles'. Who else would have cared so much about them? None of these guys seemed to, and they were born free. Funny. He would have thought it would be the other way around.

Well. If it was just to be up to him, he would accept the challenge, as he had accepted so many others in his life. He had decided long ago to follow his destiny as he felt led, and right now he knew that included doing what he could to save the eagles. He'd just have to find a way to save them without getting fired.

Willie must have come to the same conclusion, because he was already in the mess area peeling potatoes when Santos walked in. Looking up, he smiled crookedly and shrugged his shoulders. Santos grinned back, nodded wordlessly, scrubbed his hands, and grabbed a skillet.

As soon as dinner was over, they both got up and started clearing the tables. Santos had his hands full of plates when Al sidled up to him. A burly guy, gruff when he did talk, but mostly tight-lipped, he took Santos aback by leaning in toward him with a hoarse whisper, "You make pretty good grub, Santos. Hot goin' down, but sticks to the ribs." He cleared his throat and added out loud, his voice deep, a natural match to the big frame, "If you and Willie want"— he nodded toward Willie, who'd heard his name and stood up straight, wiping his hands on the towel over his shoulder as he listened in surprised gratitude—"you can go on, take off and do your thing with mama eagle. I got nothin' better to do. Might as well clean up from now on."

Throwing his arms impulsively around Al's big shoulders, Santos hugged him as tight as he could manage. "Hey, man, that is very great. *You* great! We all help now,

73

not hurt. That is the way it is meant to be! Willie, we can go now. You ready?"

"Yes, sir!" said Willie, grinning and yanking his hands out of the dishwater like a boy just told he could forget the dishes and go play ball.

As they rushed out, he was wiping them dry on his shirt. Every other man on the line was heading toward the wash bucket with his own plate, and Jake was just looking on, shaking his head, trying to frown with the corners of his lips turned up ever so slightly.

So it was that a group of men just earning their livings, doing their jobs, looking out for their own skins, their own families, their own goals, or lack of them, were awakened by one man's passion and an eagle's need. Alone, there was nothing. Together, there was all.

For the next five days, the two unlikely partners synchronized skills and devoted every break they could squeeze in to climbing the mountain and catching, carrying and tossing fish high into the air, setting a ready-made banquet table right in front of the baby eagle until finally he was able to discover his own perfect timing.

By then, they were almost like family. The two surrogate fathers held their breaths and puffed out their chests, wanting him to excel but not wanting the adventure to be over, as the huge baby bird they now called Wings dug talons into the boulder's granite and sprang up almost before the trout had left Willie's hand. Snatching it out of the air as though he'd been fishing like that all his life, he arched over backward and floated just like his mother, proudly showing off the silver trophy clasped firmly within his claws.

From their perches on the mountain, both Willie and Santos threw caution to the wind and shouted, "Yahoo! Go, Wings!" To their delight, instead of being scared off, the eaglet's mother seemed to join in, screeching what seemed to them like a joyous "Eeeeaaaah" as she leapt off the boulder and swooped right past the two men first, then up to her young, and on skyward into a victory loop.

"Well done," the young one heard. "You are almost ready."

12

Was he? Were they? They could only hope they'd done enough, soon enough. Now they had to get back in earnest to building for the future—theirs and many others'. In the great cause of progress, after all, the disintegration of many pasts would be incidental. Santos and Willie would once again become an integral part of the beast here to attack the home of those they had helped. They would ride like cowboys on the metal creature's back as its raucous bellowing became a roar of challenge. With a great belch, it would heave forward and charge onto the mountain's base.

The mountain mother was rooted deep. She could only sit in her place and adapt, as she always had done. She could only endure as a thin trail of smoke encircled her completely all the way up to her towering crest, there forming into putrid clouds of thick blackness, shutting out the light.

On another ordinary day, Santos would find himself crawling, stumbling up her gravelly slopes, trying to relax the tightness in his chest. His vision blurred through moist lashes, he fell to his knees repeatedly along the way, thrusting hot sticks into her sides as he was meant to do.

Furtively, he searched the skies, swiping at the salty wetness on his grimy cheeks. Too late to stop it now. Willie started at the top where Santos had placed the dynamite, lighting each fuse on his way.

"I hope and pray that Jake was right," Santos shouted, scrambling back down to crouch behind a truck, "about the ruckus roustin' em out in time!"

"Here's hopin' Wings is strong enough to get outa here in time!' echoed Willie, hustling down beside him.

"Fire in the hole!"

Everyone knew. But they still had to give fair warning to their fellow humans. They covered their ears against the sudden silence, and waited.

13

All morning, the eagles had been restless. The boulder beneath them had tried to be steadfast, but now even he began to shake as the cloud of noisy smoke burgeoned ever closer. Finally, he couldn't help but shimmy downward almost a foot.

The younger eagle sprang up and soared toward the open sky, calling out to his mother, "Do not worry!" she called back, lifting off to join him, "Look who is leading. You are well prepared to face what comes!"

An uneasy awareness of separation settled onto the boulder as the two mighty birds opened their wings fully and ventured out together, just as the first blast blew a gaping hole in the mountain's belly.

The noise was muffled, but loud enough to have frightened away any creature that still could escape. The two bald eagles might have sped away like rockets themselves, so endowed were they with power. But they too, like the eaglet's father, were driven by an inner voice not away from the disturbance, but toward it. This was their mountain, their valley, home, and nesting place of many generations before them. Together, they stretched their huge wingspans, each seven feet tip to tip, now forming one imposing figure in perfect rhythm, synchronized bombers shooting across the smoky blue sky. They must find the intruder, protect the territory that was theirs, claimed by their ancestors generations ago, protected to the death by her mate and his father. Instinctively, they raced forward, prepared to attack if necessary.

"Look, there they are!" shouted Santos, relieved to see the two eagles aiming their way. Still in formation, they glided majestically in a wide circle above the men, as if reviewing their subjects below and showing off Junior's maturing skills.

"Yahoo!" shouted Willie raspily, careful not to scare them.

Hushed excitement worked through the line. "They made it!" bellowed Pete, punching Santos on the shoulder. "Santos, you did it! Willie, you old dog, look at your baby go!" He elbowed Al, who slapped Andy on the back, and soon, every man on the job was cheering with abandon.

"Sshhh!"

But the eagles were already alarmed. The female suddenly screeched a warning and zoomed down toward them exactly as her mate had done. The eaglet dropped in close behind her.

"Noooo!" Santos screamed. "You suppose to get out of here, you crazy birds! Go away! Go the *other* way!" He waved at them frantically.

The men started dropping their tools to join in, one by one. Thrusting their arms up in the air, they all waved and shouted in chorus, "Noooo! Not this way, you fool birds. Shooo, shooo outa here! Git!"

They were all holding their breaths when the eagles finally broke their dives and swooped upward to circle again. "Eeeeeeee!" cried the mother bird, turning her head to gaze long and hard at Santos. *Why? Was this not the same man who had shared his food, the one who had visited them on their rock home to bring them sustenance? How could he attack them and their home now?*

The sharp arrows of her recognition sent a shiver through Santos. Had he saved them then only to draw them now toward their doom? He hadn't thought of their flying in toward the danger or so close. Hating it, almost sick, he did the only thing he could think of—he bent down, grabbed a handful of rocks, and hurled them at the eagles—not quite far enough to hit them, but just far enough to scare them away.

Confused, Mama Eagle called to Wings and coaxed him up to safer heights.

Santos yearned to explain, apologize, try to help them understand. But the moment was urgent. All he could do was scream at them desperately, "Shooo! Git! Git away!" as unashamed tears streamed down his chiseled face.

Angry now, but still confused, the eagles spiraled upward just as another blast shot bits of mountain toward them like shrapnel. Truth filtered into awareness, exploding harsh reality. Huge pieces of granite were smashed and hurled into hundreds of tiny missiles, whizzing past them, all around them in every direction. Only one more time did they recklessly dive-bomb the creature together, side by side, catapulting toward the heart of danger, the noisy hard-shelled beast. Furiously, they plunged toward the men's faces, wings flapping wildly, aiming at every man—except Santos and Willie. Perhaps they did understand. The eagles appeared to remain loyal even if they thought the men did not.

"No!" warned Santos.

"Git outa here!" shouted Willie. They waved their arms in wide arcs, as if they could move the birds to safety with invisible wands.

Eventually, the mighty birds seemed to realize even they were impotent against the combined forces of men and machines. Their cries were drowned in a wave of crashes echoing, flooding the valley. As blasts rocketed in growing crescendos of destruction, the two eagles jetted up through the mountain's halo of frothy clouds, letting out a frenzy of screams as they warned themselves and all else throughout the valley that nothing...nothing...nothing...would ever be the same.

Only they cried out. Only they had retorted noisily. All others with wings or legs had fled long ago or were fleeing now. The great mountain, still rooted in her false immortality, only sat in her place as she had to do, suffering her own upheaval with no apparent attempt at defense. In earnest now, the serpent's mouths of jagged metal began to gobble hungrily at the mountain's innards. Each load of rocks and grit, boulders and pebbles, all that formed the debris of her reduction, was lifted in triumph, hurled gloatingly toward the sky where the eagles still circled, then spat disdainfully into the cavernous mouths of trucks that stalked nearby.

More and more as the day wore on, the eagles' cries became mournful, ritualistic, reduced to a symphonic memorial. When the sun reached its peak and began to slip downward, the mother eagle finally drifted into a current that moved directly away from the mountain valley. The younger bird fell into formation just behind the tip of her right wing. Feeling the lifting tug, they straightened their necks sternly forward, ignoring the unexpected pain that seared through them as they aimed resolutely away from home.

The serpent's blasts fading behind called out the mountain's pain and loss. Perhaps if they stayed, some semblance of what had been would remain. They had become of the mountain—the mountain, the boulder throne, and its valley, of themselves. How could they leave it all even in the midst of its destruction?

But already, it was not what it once had been. A large part of their beings hung back, ripping a part from them, lingering behind even as they moved their wings up and down to go forward. Deep within, they both knew there was no more reason for looking back. Something of themselves now lay ahead.

14

s the distance between them grew, the eagles'
boulder still clutched at his place on the dwindling
mountainside, aware of a new discomfort, the
sharp bite of aloneness. The eagles' farewell cries had
pierced his granite with heavy finality. What was to be
his purpose now? Was he never again to encourage young
birds to escape from the false security of their nests, or
feel the warmth of their feathered bodies clinging to him
until the courage within them was fully awakened? Would
more eagles ever come and make him their throne, their
springboard to the skies, their refuge in storms and through
the chill of night?

All around him, the mountain was surrendering more
and more of herself. Confusion replaced order as separate
pieces, once gathered and grand with common purpose, fell
into a crowd of anonymity. Suddenly sliced into alienation,
each piece now tumbled alone one upon the other, granite

gnashing granite, torn away from that which just moments ago had seemed to be of itself.

By late afternoon, the huge metal jaws of the monster hung over the eagles' boulder. An unfamiliar pleading bled from his innermost core, a desperate cry of energy to the forces that had made him. *Please! Let me stay here lacing the side of the mountain mother, haven to the great birds, a creation of significance, fulfilling that which has always been and forever must be my purpose! Let us all be once more and forever as we were meant to be! Bring the eagles back! Put the mountain back together!*

But other forces had already come and were now at work, forcing him along in a reality that refuses to go back. Eager with its own sense of purpose, the beast opened wide its jagged teeth and closed them around the boulder, lifted his long body at a clumsy angle, and carried him to a waiting truck, where it opened again and placed him with careful precision, as if in offering, right in the center of its bed. Soon, another boulder was placed beside him, then another, then a full load of broken pieces, sharp edges scraping against his side. The deluge continued until the eagles' throne was completely buried, squeezed against his granite brothers within the strange confines of man's metal, enveloped in darkness, covered in dust. Submerged in confusion.

What force had covered the light with a hot blackness deeper than night's? Where were the breeze and its caress, the sweet bath of evening to wash the grit and dust that now caked him? *It is I, the eagle's boulder, the rock that helped to form the face of the mountain mother for centuries, open to the world,* he cried into the sudden night. *Let me be once more and forever as I was truly meant to be. A thing of significance! Take me back to where I belong. Mountain sentinel. Throne to eagles! I must remain there fulfilling my purpose as it was meant to be.*

Only the turn of the truck motor answered, as Jake gave Santos his command. "Move it out!"

Santos waved toward the window and tugged hard on the wheel, oblivious to the presence of his old friend, the eagles' throne. The truck lumbered away from what remained of the wounded mountain. Snaking its way through her middle was the beginning of a tunnel that would ease man's journey though rock and clay valleys instead of across slippery mountain roads.

As it was meant to do, the truck pushed farther and farther away from the mountain, heaving its load of rocks and boulders toward the waiting ocean. The ball of fire rose high in the sky above them, then dropped behind them again and again as the truck started and stopped, resuming with every new dawn its relentless forward march. The eagle's gold-flecked granite throne was on the bottom layer, buried in constant darkness by other remnants of the mountain mother. The crushing weight of many others, both larger and smaller than he, bore down upon him, smashing his once-proud face against the hot metal bed of the rusty truck.

Was this to be his existence now, this seething blackness, this smothering closeness with no familiar sense of joining? This pressure that threatened to burst him from within? This empty sense of belonging nowhere? Obviously, he was here. But what was here, where was here? Where were they? He only knew there seemed to be no escape from what must have been a colossal error of fate. All the while, he cried out to whatever forces could hear him, "Stop! Turn around! Take me back!"

But the truck kept moving forward, bearing its heavy groaning load all the way to its destination of Sand Harbor. Only there on the sand did it creak to a stop, back up, lift its bed, and belch forth its burden along the shore of a magnificent body of water. The boulder felt itself jolted into the grinding eye of a great thunder, disjointed pieces of the mountain's innards tumbling with him, slamming his surface suddenly into the cold, wet sand, jarring him to the core.

Ah, a flash of light! Relief!

But soon, a harsh slap of dampness was falling upon him, completely covering him! The entire universe seemed to be crushing him beneath its weight.

Then stillness once more, completely surrounding him. He was buried again completely. There seemed to be nothing else. Only total burial. It seemed as if he had ceased to be. Somehow, the long, flat boulder was still aware. But only of nothingness now. *All the more terrible! Nothingness!*

He could endure it no more. The once-proud throne to eagles gave up. He simply turned inward unto himself. It was the only direction open to his choosing. He began to close his pores to all awareness of the now and immersed himself instead in his own sense of eternity, as it always had been—but never really would be.

Before long, the large mass of rock energy had numbed himself in the haze of a blissful past within his own imaginings. Once again, he was firmly lacing the side of the mountain mother. His destiny was solid. His existence was significant after all, and forevermore. He was filled with the purpose that was only his. Always it would be so with the justice of continuing. As it was surely meant to be.

15

There was no turning inward or back for the eagles. Resolutely, they propelled their sleek bodies, hers shiny black with white head and tail, his still rough and tousled-looking, brown feathers streaked with black. On through the center of a vast and ever-changing new world, they moved. The familiar song, which had once been the very essence of their existence, settled into a soft, distant hum, always present, and yet no more, other than within. Now they danced through the skies to the music of zest, an ovation of colorful life and promise beckoning them forward. Somewhere, there were others like themselves, catching the waves of motion, traveling through the open space that was theirs for the using with a bristling excitement akin to their own.

The skill and strength of the eaglet was increasing daily as he followed his mother with cautious bravado across the skies, absorbing crucial lessons along the way. They rested often, completely motionless, conserving the heat of their bodies and rekindling the sparks that would light their way for the long journey. Aiming her energies always toward survival for two, the she-eagle was ever mindful of encroaching unawares upon other eagles' territory, invisibly but forcefully fenced in the air. Wizened by experience, she was all too aware that adult eagles would meet the challenge of death head-on to protect their nesting and feeding grounds, just as her mate had done.

As she knew he would have done naturally by now in ordinary days, the mother expected the eaglet to claim his independence from her more completely at Eagle Island, where salmon and trout displayed themselves openly, inviting the snug embrace of a raptor's quick talons. Where food was so plentiful, many others like themselves wintered in relative harmony with no need for territories. She looked forward to exchanging the task of preening for mites. Unattended, the pesky little bugs could drain the mightiest bird's strength. They assured their own survival by attending to each others' needs with essential ritual.

The vision in her mind's eye brought warmth and lightness to her breast. She picked up speed, calling out, "Ahhh, come young one! It won't be long now! We draw closer, day by day!" Smoothly, the young male moved up beside her. Side by side, they aimed farther and farther away from the mountain that was no more, aiming together toward a new future.

16

At the same moment, Santos was turning the steering wheel firmly away from the ocean, leaving the eagles' boulder behind. The truck felt infinitely lighter beneath him, almost leaping over scattered rocks, cutting through thick sand with ease, as he angled toward the heart of town—and the post office. It seemed so long ago, when he'd jumped excitedly off the train, the zest of new freedom shining in his eyes as he'd first shook hands with Jake and Willie and Al.

He smiled at the memory of the naive young man he had been such a short time ago. He was far wiser now—*yes, yes, but also a bit more weary*, he thought. Now he knew that, yes, America held the promise of freedom he had hoped for. But not as a present handed to you as soon as you got here like some in his homeland seemed to think. More like a present you had to find first with lots of wrappings and very much complication and work to untie the ribbon and tear off all the paper to get to it. Maybe it was just life, not just America, that kept the contents of that box locked away in such mystery. Like anything worthwhile, it did not come easy. Many never seemed to find it. Perhaps Santos was more determined than they. Perhaps just more in tune with his sense of purpose, the gift he had promised God he would honor and use to the best of his ability.

"Freedom don't just hand you dreams," he had written Marcella from camp. "It just lets you figure everything out for yourself, first to find some way to work very hard, and then find some way you can only hope you open your own gift someday. Maybe you get lucky. Maybe you don't. Maybe you give up and go for the siesta. But at least here you have the chance to try. Here you are free to try to be everything you are meant to be. Soon you all come here, and we learn together, and then we all go home and show Cuba how to do it." He knew none of them would ever abandon their biggest dream of all—a free Cuba.

The spring in his step belied the weariness he felt as Santos drew near to the post office clutching the tiny key that held all the power in his world in this moment. Soon, a shower and a juicy red steak would energize his body. For now, the vision of a letter he hoped would be there was sparking his soul.

The small door opened, and Santos took a deep breath, filling his nostrils, his lungs, his very soul with the scents that emanated from the little box. With his eyes closed, he would have known. Here she was in front of him, the perfume of gardenias, along with garlic from the kitchen, tobacco from the field. It was as if his whole family had appeared in front of him here to embrace and encourage him.

"My dear Santos," the letter began. "It is with great happiness that I shout across the seas, so relieved to know you are still okay, that no harm has come to you. I thank God every day, first that you made it safely there, and then that you stay safe and well. I am so proud you work so hard, and now you try for the citizenship! May God and His angels continue to watch over you as He did along your journey. There, in America, you will surely find the path that is yours alone, leading to your destiny and everything you were meant to be…"

Santos closed the mailbox door, turned the key, dropped it carefully back into his pocket, and started walking toward Sand Harbor Steaks 'n Burgers, his eyes and heart still glued to the soggy paper in his hand.

"We await, your Mama', your Papa', and I, for the most happy day when you will be able to send for us or come for us, and we can join you there in freedom, too. It's okay if we have to work hard. You know we are no strangers to very hard work. And it is okay too, we don't mind smelly boats and hiding under the stinky fishnets if that is our fate! But hurry, Santos, if you can! Manuel's papa has not been seen in town since the Sunday after Manuel defected from the Cuban team while they were playing the baseball there in Miami. Perhaps it is just coincidence and not the same anyway. No cause for fear. Yet we all know of your own special talent. This too, will be sorely missed by the one who calls himself our Maximum Leader."

A shiver moved up Santos' back like an army of ants, and he had to stop reading for a minute. Squeezing his eyes shut, he whispered, "Please, God. You will protect them, yes? This is your plan, is it not? America for us all, this is right? It is okay I am here first?"

He never would have dreamed it would take so long. First, the money, a little room to call home, a long line and a job, a long line to become the citizen someday. If only they all could have come together. But the secret boat had had enough room for only one stowaway—and even under the cloak of darkness, to move so many people across the Cuban streets, then through the woods and the marsh, moving only at night—just to get to it would have been far too dangerous.

Trembling fingers fumbled toward his back pocket and found the big handkerchief, once white, now dingy gray. Mama' had presented it to him so lovingly the night before he left, as if it were a gold watch. He'd made a point of accepting it in like manner, holding it against his face for a long, deep whiff. "Ah, Mama', it smells of you," he'd said. "I will carry it always and think of home." She'd reached up, her arms stretching hard, and he'd bent down and hugged her so tightly her heels had lifted off the floor just as he'd been doing since his fifteenth birthday. Even Papa', usually offering only gruff shoulder hugs, had enveloped him fully in his arms that night.

Dabbing nervously at his forehead, he read on, picturing Marcella's long dark hair draping onto the paper. She'd probably had to hold it back with her left hand so she could write: "You are missed by many, Santos—but none as much as by me, your adoring Marcella. Every night, I watch the lion of courage leap across the black sky and take comfort knowing that you can see him too from where you are. Such a big world, and yet so small! So far apart, and yet close enough to see the same stars and make wishes upon them together, even if not at the same time and place."

Santos read her words again and again as he waited for his steak. Normally, all of his senses would have zeroed in on the fat, juicy cut of tender red meat as soon as the waitress set it sizzling before him. But tonight, his eyes darted only briefly away from the letter when he couldn't cut and spear a bite now and then without looking. When he finally folded the letter over that night, reluctantly closing his eyes to sleep, the paper and his cheeks were damp, and every word had been seared into his memory. As he drifted off, he and Marcella were reaching across a broiling sea toward each other, the tips of their fingers touching as they had the night he'd left her on the shore. He knew now they would be connected always, no matter the distance between them. How warm it made him feel, sensing the closeness she marveled at!

It was not so pleasant being reminded that ripping a road through a mountain's belly was not the path to his destiny. His hands were meant to paint, to draw, to widen the narrow vision of other men by memorializing God's beauty on paper and velvet. He had come here for the chance to do that, to avoid the politico's clutches, to express his own feelings, not theirs! His family would regret to know that that sort of freedom still escaped him. But even more, they would regret his inability to send for them.

And so, early the next morning, the artist's hands, now burly and rough, gripped the steering wheel with new resolve and turned the truck eastward, back toward the mountain. He had thought of not going back, of staying here by the water to paint. But dreams must be patient. Though his soul was conflicted with the sure knowledge that he was meant to create, urgency demanded that Santos continue to do just the opposite, at least for now. His heavy heart lifted, he shouted toward the sunrise.

"Mañana! I will hold you in my arms, Marcella. This day, I make my way again to the mountain. Next day soon, you and Mama' and Papa' make your way to America. I will come for you! It is not quite home. But it is free. The way is not so easy either. But it is free. You will see for yourselves very soon. Someday soon, some tomorrow soon, you will all understand like me."

He rolled down the window and sang out loud, his voice bouncing with the tires as he gassed the truck harder, pushing it over ruts and gullies.

"Mañana! Mañana. Mañana is good enough for me. Mañana…"

Before he'd even reached the halfway point where the trees thickened and the air cooled, he had to sing louder, though his voice grew hoarse, to drown out the growing buzz in his head, *What if something does happen to them? What if the guard pounds on the door of their little house in the middle of some night, and the neighbors all huddle, trembling and afraid to help when they hear the sounds, maybe even booted toes and rifle butts forcing the door open so soldiers of the* revolución *could yank my poor little mama' and papa' out of their beds and cart them away?* They would not go easily, he knew. Mama' might try to kick at their shins, and Papa' might never stop the resisting until it could be too late. What if they were beaten, or even just locked away from the open world all of their remaining days and nights? All because of him! Would he, Santos, runaway son, know in his heart what had happened, and when? Would Marcella be able to get word to him? What if none of them could ever join him in America?

Santos leaned his head out the window, raising his free hand toward heaven with open palm, imploring, "This is what You want, is it right? I am not loco, yes? You give me gift to use for You, for the peoples, not for the politicos, the revolución, is it right? I am to make good use of this gift from You? But here I am, going on my way back to rip out more of the mountain's belly. This is *Your* mountain, is it not? You want that I should do this? Better I should have stayed by the shore from the start and paint, even to beg for the food? Yet, it is I, Santos, who is needing my family, the sooner the better, or else. Tell me, what am I to do?"

For miles, his mind roiled constantly like the sea itself. The ball of fire rose in the sky, beckoning him steadily toward the mountain, as it was surely meant to do.

Then, suddenly, a huge cloud moved across the sun, blotting it out. A soft mist began drifting onto the windshield. Santos tensed, hardly able to find the road through the blur of wet dust. He kept squinting, gazing more at the glass than through it, until the drifting mist became rain and began washing the heavy dust off the truck. When the glass was wet enough not to smear too much, Santos turned on the wipers.

There it danced before him, another miracle sent to soothe him, as clear as could be, right before his blinking eyes—a huge rainbow, like none he'd ever seen in his life! It arched from one side of the mountain range circle all the way across to the other side, like a rainbow handle holding up a giant Easter basket.

If Santos had had a canvas with him, and brilliant oils, he would have stopped right there to try to capture God's beauty, though he could never do it justice, so that everyone in the world could see what he was privileged enough to witness right this moment—even if he'd had to drive back to camp in the dark and lose sleep. He rolled down the window and leaned his head out, letting the rain wash over him, laughing out loud as he shouted, "Man! You don' jus' send the answer over time and hope I get it, maybe! You hit Santos over the head with the rainbow! Ha! Ha!"

. Laughing right out loud, he pushed harder on the gas pedal. He would hurry now and do what he had to do so that he could finally do what he *must*! His mind's eye cast right in the middle of the rainbow as he drove toward it the very last image he'd had of Wings and Mama Eagle, flying away as he'd watched them grow smaller and smaller, two dots in the distance, until they were out of sight.

He'd thought he would never forget exactly how they'd looked and behaved, every cock of their heads, every shade of color in their shiny feathers. But it had only been a couple of weeks since he'd seen them last, and already, the image in his mind had faded. Now, picturing them there, in the bowl of the rainbow, Santos vowed to paint the eagles just like that, before they disappeared into the horizon of his mind's eye completely.

His thoughts were moving like waves again, excited and eager, like the sea racing always toward shore. Eventually, the rain slowed, the rainbow disappeared, and the ball of fire rose higher again, beckoning him steadily toward the mountain, as it was surely meant to do on this ordinary day. The mountain was still waiting to be moved.

As they also were meant to do, the two eagles were aiming away from it. The same ball of fire that beckoned

Santos toward it cast its warming gleam on the feathers of their wings as they flew toward Eagle Island. At the same moment, it shot a generous shaft of light on the only edge of the eagles' boulder that was not buried in the sand beneath his granite brothers.

17

With the flickering beacon of life resumed, a faint whirring stirred the boulder's senses. Pressures began to be lifted. Crisp, salt air sifted through the dust and touched his surface. Timidly, the eagle's boulder dared to open his pores, very slowly, to a growing expectation. Had the siege of change passed? Was he still at home on the mountain, after all, where he was meant to be?

But, no! A long shadow worked its clumsy way toward him. It fell across him. Quickly, he tried to escape once more to find the comforting hiding place within. He should never have opened to vulnerability, never! Not in this strange, foreboding place. But too late! Again, the boulder felt the steel jaws closing around him, the crunching, clenching jaws of confinement carrying him against his choosing. He was yanked upward and then reeling through the soggy air.

"Take me back!" he tried to cry out. "Take me back to life itself, to things as they were, as they are meant to be! Allow me to fulfill my purpose!"

Instead, the metal teeth bit into his side and swung him across other boulders strewn out beneath him, all shapes and sizes. The boulder felt himself being lowered. The jaws released their hold. He braced again for a hard landing; instead, he was placed ever so gently, right in the midst of other boulders, as if being presented to them as a fragile gift.

The dust settled with a hush. The crane creaked away into the distance. A spray of softness bathed the full expanse of the eagles' rock, rushing a chilled cleansing through his pores and into his core. The ball of fire was high now, a huge ornament hanging in a bright blue sky above him, offering again its illusion of protection, a shield of constancy, of continuing. Had he been heard after all?

A swell of vibrations rose up all around him. "Hurray! At last, there is light. We are here!" The cries came from the same remnants of the mountain he had suffered the long, dark journey with, away from what they had all been together.

"Here?" the eagles' boulder cried. "Where is here? I belong where the mighty eagles soar and bask in the sun on my back in the mountain valley. The royal young are supposed to grow strong upon my back on the mountain! That is where I need to be. Are we there, back where we belong, on the mountain? It doesn't feel the same!"

As if in reply, a bold wave reached up and slapped him with the open hand of reality. For the first time, he became aware of being perched on the side of a high rock mass almost surrounded by water. Joining to form a large finger, the boulders, which had once helped to form a mountain, now pointed collectively out from the sand into a vast and powerful world of wetness.

"Hurrah for purpose renewed!" the rocks around him shouted in chorus. "Once more, our purpose is known, our noble existence to be fulfilled. Again, we are where we belong."

"I am meant to be lacing the side of the mountain mother, throne and refuge to the mighty eagle, not a bunch of rocks by this endless, noisy water! How can I fulfill such a noble purpose here?"

"You squeak with the naïveté of a pebble," roared the boulder next to him, rounder but of similar mass. "We are the same. We are still of noble purpose. We are just in a different place now! Our purpose here is to halt the onslaught of these chiseling waters from the harbor."

"I see no purpose in this existence," cried the eagle's boulder. "I was meant to be, but this was not. The fates have erred. I do not belong here. Where is the mountain? Where are the eagles? I will not be fulfilled here."

Again, a wave lifted up and cracked down over all of them, shaking them through to the very core. His neighbor was not dissuaded. "In refusing the truth of reality, you refuse the fulfillment you clamor for," he warned. "Here you are also helping to form the side of a mountain. Your purpose is grand. Once more, you are privileged to the sensations of air and water and sunlight. You were not meant to be a throne forever. Humble yourself! Open yourself to all that is offered, here and now, and in so doing, be fulfilled. Discover your victory here!"

But victory is born in the heart of existence. The eagles' rock began closing his pores, shutting the others out, reciting over and over to himself, "Things will be once more as they were always meant to be. I will not acquiesce, as my fickle brothers have done. I will be once more as I was meant to be, where I was meant to be. I simply must wish harder..."

As the ball of fire slipped downward, and the moon took its place in the sky, the eagles' boulder began to realize he had not even been aware of the full sweetness of his mountain world until he'd been wrenched away from it. He had come to assume that being there was his right and his place, the unquestioned purpose for his existence. Having known nothing else, felt nothing else, the possibility of such drastic loss and change had never dawned on him. Perhaps this was punishment for his lack, to be trapped in a place in which he was strange even to himself, beyond his own comprehension and acceptance.

New dawns and sunsets brought no relief, no adjustment. The air still felt foreign, filling the boulder's gold-flecked pores with cold and constant moisture. Odd, clawed creatures skittered across him, scrambled beneath him, darted from him in pursuit of prey. Human feet scratched incessantly across his upturned face.

He cried out to the forces that had made him, to plead for the recycling of time in his behalf, "Take me back where I belong, to the mountain valley!"

The eagles' boulder heard in reply to his ongoing cries only the whooshing noise that rhythmically attacked the silence of the peace he sought, as days were born and died with the night and were born again in the name of time, relentlessly pursuing the existence and passing of itself.

18

The rhythm of the eagles' days, as smooth and firm as the powerful thrust of their wings, followed, as always, the constant beat of search and conquest, a pulse akin to their rippling beings. They had gone far and seen much since leaving the mountain. More and more surely, the eaglet was learning to swoop in behind his mother toward quick rushes in the grass and thus assure their sustenance. Together, the hunt was so much easier, but as time went on, they both knew he could do it alone if he had to.

Still, there was more than the drive for survival, the primal need to fill their crops. Beating deep within the two hearts was a building desire that compelled them on toward communion with others. Everything was as it should be for now.

And yet, a vague discontent began to simmer within the adult, confusing her indomitable spirit. Though sharing the skies and the trees and the kill, she struggled to quell a rising sense of aloneness within, an awareness of purpose still unfulfilled. Nevertheless. Could one sense of purpose extinguish another? And so, day after day, she thrust her neck sternly forward and aimed her beak resolutely toward the south, leading her young as she was meant to do toward a shared destiny. Everything was straight ahead, waiting for them at Eagle Island.

The two had come to rest in a tall pine when, from the horizon, she saw a floating spot grow near and take on the shape of another like them. She cocked her head, aimed the bead of a golden eye toward the shape, and watched the smooth gliding that drew the spread of wings and tail and white, rounded head ever nearer. Her pulse quickened. Tail feathers stirred. An invisible magnet tugged at her.

Wings sensed his mother's excitement. Tightening his grip on the branch they shared, he stayed put as she answered the unexpected call and pushed off, leaving him behind. Watching in awe, he tensed as she plummeted, spiraling down from the pine. It seemed she would smash right into the earth, a death dive of passion he was yet to understand. The other bird was now directly overhead. Barely in time, the she-eagle widened the spread of her wings, fixed just the right portion of tail feathers into a strong but delicate bend, and slid upward on a trail of air.

A joyous squawk escaped her throat as she allowed herself to be carried up, up to the other's level and beyond to form a slow, graceful arc as she fell backward. Behind and beneath, up through the trail of his forward path she looped. At first, he seemed undaunted, unimpressed, and flapped his wings in lazy response. She slid sideward and circled him with curls of flight.

Suddenly, he darted upward. Leveling off just above her, he began to match the floating tease of her game. He was mesmerized. All else faded as the midday sun played its brightness along the imposing stretch of her sleek body and bounced a gleam off the band of blackness that ruffled up to her white neck and head. On through the afternoon, they swam a cloverleaf of air, together, apart, away, and toward, each exhibiting for the other. Her rhythm became his rhythm, his, hers, as they beat the sky with their wings in proclamation of mutual choice.

The young eagle, now suddenly alone, could only watch. He knew instinctively that joining their dance would be an intrusion. When the clouds were heavy with the day's dusty color, she suddenly dashed away from him, leaving the trail of her call behind, as she projected herself toward the edging of pines on the opposite side of the clearing. Quickly, the adult male mounted the wake of her flight and their destiny, away from the mother's young eaglet. How far they would go, or in which direction, or even if they would go farther at all, was suddenly unimportant. In the very center of her, everything was as it should be, and that was all that mattered. It was time for her brash young one to mark his own path through the skies.

And so into the night, the once-brazen eaglet remained on the branch, transfixed by yet another unexpected change, a sudden shroud of solitude that chilled his bones. Now, only briefly, he appeared as a lone, dark, brooding figure, mourning his loss. Yet he knew, as his mother knew, this time was different. The undoing of her first mate's destiny had been a thing to mourn. This was to be purpose fulfilled for both of them.

Alone, he perched through the night taking his rest, telling himself that everything was as it should be. At the first wisp of light the next morning, he pushed away from the pine, never looking back, and resumed his journey in the same direction toward Eagle Island, and his destiny.

19

Visions of an island of eagles were with Santos as well every morning when he first turned over on his cot, trying not to wake up. The dreams were always better than reality, majestic wings rushing overhead to welcome him to freedom. But then, every morning, there he was, splashing his face with frigid stream water out of a cold, steel pan. Sometimes, catching a glimpse of himself in the water, he wondered if Marcella would still love him, or even recognize him, with the rough skin of his gaunt face half-covered with coarse black hair. Shaving was too much trouble out here. Besides, it had taken so long for the goose bumps to settle down after his first morning's splash, he'd decided right then and there to let his beard grow to shut out the chill. Was this the freedom he had sought so desperately?

But it wouldn't be too much longer now. He'd signed on to work six days a week, sunup to sunset, to hasten toward the real goal. He could concentrate more on the job now, since that poignant day when Mama Eagle and Wings had claimed their own freedom, their own future, leaving what once had been behind.

As their memory faded into the background of his daily challenges, Santos could only hope they'd survived. Every once in a while, Willie would sidle up to him and throw an arm around his shoulder, reminding him of the adventure they'd shared. "Reckon those big birds are out there somewhere havin' the time of their lives," he'd brag. "Think they ever watch for flyin' fish?"

The first time he'd said it, Santos had doubled over, laughing at the image of the eaglet missing, then pouncing on the fish on the ground. Whether Willie forgot he'd said it the first time, or just liked to relive the excitement, he'd ask the same question every time he got the chance. From the third time on, Santos just winked and nodded obligingly, "I think, yes."

"Hope we didn't mess Junior up for life, like my pa messed up my head!" Willie surprised him by adding dolefully one day, rubbing his own beard of oddly mixed red and gray.

Santos stifled the urge to paint Willie and his beard on the spot. "I think Wings is fat and happy. But what did your papa do to your head?"

"More like on it than in it," muttered Willie, trying to maintain his tough demeanor. "Hit me up side of it, now and then, to keep me in line. On the head and about everywhere else, wherever he could reach without too much trouble."

"Ayyyyy," whispered Santos, whittling at a stick. His own papa' used to shape kitchen chairs out of sticks such as these. Always he was building, not tearing down. For this, Santos would forever be grateful. "That is too bad. Too bad for you and for your pa. Too bad for all that he touched."

"Yup," said Willie, breathing in as he said it. "Truth be told, I reckon Pa didn't have much respect for nobody or nothing." He tried to swipe across his eyes fast enough that it might not be noticed by Santos, who was staring out at the horizon. "Guess that's why I didn't either, and why I was so quick to want to hurt that baby eagle's daddy, when he came at us the way he did."

"Ahhh, Willie! That was sadly unfortunate, yes. But it is all behind us now, as we rest from our labor, and the eagles fly, all in the freedom that God has intended," Santos assured him, leaning his chair back against a tree. He seemed to be studying the sunset, but his mind was deep in contemplation, *So much pain, for no good reason.* For a long time, he rolled his head from side to side against the tree, comforted somehow by the roughness of its bark. Finally, he breathed in softly and added, "It is time to put this pain behind you, Willie, like our friends, the eagles. Your own destiny lies ahead. The same as the eagles' and mine. We must do our best to soar with the wings we are given, my friend."

Willie snorted. "Easy for you to say. Can't figure as I expect the good Lord has any big purpose for me to fulfill." Just as Santos was about to object, he added, "But you're right about one thing. I reckon you can call me your friend any time. Thanks for showin' me another way to be." He'd blurted out the last words, hurrying them out of his chest and his mouth to keep his voice from choking.

Santos placed the palm of his big hand square in the middle of Willie's back and held it there for about five minutes. In another shared epiphany, neither man disturbed the silence with more words—one more would have been too many.

20

A growing bond was being celebrated on the breakfront, as well, with the recognition and acceptance of new purpose fanning out, boulder to boulder. Every day, a grander lilt arose, greeting the morning sun. Settling firmly into place, the newly gathered boulders truly began to form a breakfront wall of increasing solidity. They greeted each day's morning sun with a grander lilt of harmony.

But the eagles' boulder still had not joined them, other than with his outward presence, not of his own choosing. The majesty of his former self was gone, for he'd planted himself in the sterile soil of isolation, cultivating only a bitter anguish that slowly began to consume him. With every tide that brought bold, high-reaching waves slapping at him with icy precision, the boulder closed yet another pore to his environment. Eventually, his repulsion was so intense that he denounced all granite, even his own, as no more solid than quicksilver.

"Better to be of feather like the shimmering gulls that catch the waves of air all around me so effortlessly!" he cried out to whatever forces had made him. "Better that my jagged edges should extend themselves into wings and lift me to the freedom that is theirs! Better to have a choice, at least, to be significant in the scheme of things, as I was on the mountain! Why did you remove me, was I not sufficient? How long must I stay here?"

His answer came through many tides as the gold-flecked throne to eagles remained a prisoner on the jetty. Gathered droplets of energy dancing to the rhythm of their own purpose thrashed his surface constantly, building eternal puddles that worked their wetness down to his core and cut at him with trickles of dampness. No wings or feathers adorned him. Only pesky shells clung to his sides and sucked at his surface incessantly.

It wasn't long before the eagle's boulder became less than he had been, not just outside, but inside as well, as his very core was eaten away by his self-formed acid. That which remained now reached out not to help, but to hurt, to spew fumes of angry rejection against all that surrounded him and thus seemed to contribute to his plight. He began to find contorted pleasure in trying to repel from him, rather than draw toward him as he had on the mountain, utilizing the full concentration of his negative energy against anything that touched him, or dared try.

21

The young eagle, on the other hand, searched the skies as he soared across them, seeking to draw toward him, not away. For the first time, he was truly alone, not just for a night or a day, but truly alone. There was no parent to feed him, or lead him in flight, or to help him hunt for his continuing.

The lush green of pine and oak trees was scarce now, giving way to tall palm trees. There were no leafy branches like those that had beckoned him to stop along the way. He would have to find another place to rest. Somehow, he must fill his crop, regain his strength, and continue forward until he had reached the sandy shelter in the great body of water, the community he had heard of, sharing with others like himself the security of mutual support, helping to rid each other of these pesky mites that nibbled at him!

But the easy path he had traveled with his mother suddenly seemed more difficult. Was he still riding the airwaves that would lead to Eagle Island? He seemed to be getting nowhere. He had accepted his mother's determination as his own. He knew no other way. Alone, his determination began to waver.

He was soaring low, keen eyes scanning the yellow wave of ground for the gray-brown streak of potential feed when a crosscurrent tugged at the tip of his left wing and rippled across his chest, flaunting a promised thrill. Wings had tried to heed all such biddings once, to fling his youth to as many quick forays as beckoned across his world, a weightless kite freely catching every breeze. His mother was not there to caution him now. His focus weakened. He leaned into the tempting massage. Only for a fleeting moment!

The current was a wide ribbon, entwining him, pulling him away in a new direction. Where would it lead him? Before he knew it, he was floating with it, pulled away from the direction of Eagle Island with little effort. Visions of the mountain, and all that had been through many generations, had faded from his memory now. With no one to care for but himself, what was his purpose in continuing in the same direction? Yes, he was growing weaker. He needed to be rid of these mites. But perhaps there were other eagles along this new route, too. He could easily find his way to Eagle Island later. When he was ready, he would dive sharply down and quickly escape the enticing grip of this lustrous stream of air. He would drift in indulgent surrender here just a little while longer.

22

Even though they had witnessed daily the mountain's changing identity and contributed to the mountain's demise, Santos and Willie were taken aback every time they returned from wherever they'd carted the latest part of her. Right through her middle, a wide road was taking form. The mountain now resembled a big hill, rising up on each side of the road, strewn with rocks and brush here and there along her barren sides. The mountain was no longer the thing. The road was the thing.

Somewhere, they had crossed over from destroying to building. Their way was being laid before them, as men and machines made their mark on the mountain. They'd be changing many lives for the better with this road. They could see it again now.

Santos was smiling more. With no rent or food to buy, and working six days a week, his savings were growing quickly. "Not much longer, my friend! My little chiquita will be by my side to dance to our music close to me, as only Marcella can dance!"

Willie looked at him wistfully. "Yeah, it won't be that much longer," he agreed. "I hope I get to meet this Marcella. She sounds like something to work for! Maybe you two will show me how to rhumba!"

"Yes? Tell you what! I show you myself. Time to celebrate, anyway. Why spend the whole weekend here? You wanna go dance tonight?"

Willie stepped back. "Naw, I was just kiddin', man, I don't dance! I watch."

"Ayyy, carrumba, you are chicken? You don' dance?"

" You mean Willie's scared to do a little cha-cha?" chided Pete from a few feet behind them on the road, thrusting his arms toward the sky and wiggling his hips.

"You're durned right, I am," said Willie. "Plan to stay that way, too!"

Santos laughed loudly, signaling the other workers to join in. "Ayyyy, not if we have somethin' to say about it! We start teachin' tonight! Right, men? We all teach Willie to cha-cha tonight?"

"Right!" yelled Al, and then Pete, and then Andy. Before long, every man on the line was singsonging and swaying along the road with exaggerated hip movements, chiding, "Wil-l-l-lie! Wil-l-l-lie! Willie don't cha-cha! Willie don't cha-cha!"

Willie swung his pick harder, his face burning redder, until finally he thought, *If you can't beat 'em, join 'em.* He stood up straight and grinned slyly, "How 'bout a conga line? Would that satisfy you guys? All of us, tonight! In the conga line at Havana Cabana! You gotta do it, too, you know, you can't just put it out!"

Santos was the first to change the chant, feeling a tiny bit of remorse for what he'd gotten Willie into. "Conga! Conga! Every man for the Conga! Cha-cha! Samba! Every man for Conga!"

The bond had grown strong among them all. None had sought or expected it. Perhaps it was their shared purpose, day-by-day, working toward a common goal, albeit each for his own. Perhaps it was the eagles and the growth of a common caring. At any rate, when the day's work was done, and they'd made a modest attempt at a soapy splash, each man jumped into the rusty bed of a big dump truck together, all the different shapes and sizes of men this time, instead of rocks and boulders jostling against each other. Without knowing it, they, too, had become a part of the mountain, even as they altered her existence forever.

It was only natural that Santos should joyously suggest they all go out on the breakfront together, while it was still light, before dancing. "This is the place where I leave the first parts of the mountain," he announced. "Right here on the sand. You think they are all out there now?"

"Yup," said Willie, sucking in his breath as he pronounced the word, as he often did.

"We are very powerful!" boasted Santos. "Mountain, one day. Next day, jetty." He shook his head, not sure if he was proud or ashamed of the accomplishment.

"Sure don't look like a mountain now, you're right about that," said Hank.

"Ever wonder about that boulder the eagles used to stand on?" Willie yelled over his shoulder as they hiked out over the rocks. "You think he's out here, too?"

"No tellin'," mumbled Al. "I never saw it the way you did, but I doubt it's what it used to be. Probably got pulverized, with all that blasting we did."

Santos didn't admit he'd thought a lot about the eagles' boulder. He'd never tell them out loud he'd been hoping to find it, and that was really why he'd come out here. Out loud, he proclaimed, "No, that boulder has not changed. He is still big and beautiful! What you bet we walk upon him this very minute!"

While they all laughed and joked about it, Santos scanned the top layer of the breakfront, where logic told him the boulder must be, considering the timing of the drop. Just as he thought he might have caught a familiar glimpse of a golden sparkle picked up by the setting sun along the breakfront's side, Hank bellowed at them from the sand, "Come on! Don't forget why we came! Conga! Rhumba! Cha-cha-cha!" They all started chanting in unison, "Conga!

Rhumba! Cha-cha-cha!" Grabbing each other's waists, they formed an awkward Conga line and headed back over the rocks toward Hank.

Santos gave up and hustled to join them. "Nah, I'd rather samba some rhumba!" he hollered.

In a tight group, they headed for the nightclub around the corner, the one where the music sang out in Latin rhythms, twining around and through the glowing letters of red and green outside, beckoning all who passed to surrender to their own indulgence and enter. Laughing, jostling each other, enjoying a growing camaraderie, the road builders headed inside.

23

Surrounded by those that no longer bothered to acknowledge his existence, the long, flat hulk of granite remained alone. Night joined him with its darkness. He had felt the energy of the man's searching eyes as they'd focused on him briefly. Perhaps there had been a rekindling of recognition, known energies that had once touched the boulder, if only for fleeting moments, when he'd laced the side of the mountain mother. Those vibrations had been pleasant, shared happily by his eagles. They seeped again into the boulder's closed pores, teasing at him to open up.

Then, suddenly, he felt the awareness of other energies left behind by those just here, the same energies that had struck so forcefully together, rendering such violent change to him and all those around him. The eagles were gone, and so was the mountain. So was he, against his will. Even the one who had once brought life to the eagles, who had so caringly touched his own surface, had eventually been the one to cart him so roughly away and dump him here on the sand, in this strange world. Now this same man moved about so freely with the others, almost tauntingly! Was he no longer aware of the boulder's existence? Once, he had been so significant as throne to the eagle! Now they hadn't even noticed he was here. The eagles' boulder again began to close all his pores to awareness. He could not accept this wretched existence, or those who had caused it to be.

Inside the bar, Santos was acutely aware of his own energies. The deepest part of him was not in harmony here. Though he laughed as loud, danced more, drank almost as much as his compadres, he felt drained and tired inside.

"Love the way you move," slurred the tall one he had just escorted back to the table where all her friends sat with similar smiles. In fact, Santos noted, they all looked alike to him, despite different hairdos and dresses. Instead of sitting back down in the chair he'd pulled out for her, she followed him back to his seat at the bar. Her russet hair hung long and straight around her shoulders and back, struggling against the brightness of her red dress. It was tight and short, too revealing as she leaned brazenly against him, stroking his arm.

"So where are you taking this muscular body of yours for the night, when it's finally samba'd out?" she cooed.

A blithe answer was on his lips, one that would have kept the conversation going. She lowered her eyes to study his chest. The words stuck in his throat as he watched her raise them with exaggerated drama, then slowly open them wide to stare deeply into his.

He couldn't help stifling a laugh. It was all he could do to keep from laughing right out loud, as the caricature of this temptress drew itself in his mind. Cupping his big hand over hers, he pulled it down away from his chest and firmly placed it on the counter, patting it gently.

"I go where my compadres go," he announced. "But later." Sidling away from the bar, he grinned and backed toward the door. "After I go to the post-office box to see if my sweetheart is ready to come to America soon!"

Bursting outdoors, he faced the ocean and stood, legs apart, head back, eyes closed, arms out by his sides, inviting the salty mist to cleanse him inside and out. Sensing Marcella's radiant smile as he pictured her riding on the lion's back across the sky toward him, he turned in the direction of the post office, fumbled in his pocket for the key, and wrapped his long fingers lovingly around it. "Yeah? You proud of me? Me too!" he tried to shout across the ocean.

Small separate waves reached out and joined hands, running red rover toward him, recalling to him the games of his youth. Fascinated, he stopped to watch as they curtsied at him again and again. In the distance, the moon played brightly on the jetty's wet granite, frolicking to the same game. Santos felt himself being drawn once again toward the breakfront, where they'd all hiked earlier. Perhaps the light of the moon would reveal the hiding place of his old granite friend. He knew it was out here somewhere!

His shoes squished and his trousers dripped by the time he raised his leg to step on the eagles' boulder. He'd made it all the way down to the end and back, playing at dodging the waves that splashed up over the rocks.

"Yoo-hoo! Eagle's Rock! You out here?" he shouted into the thundering night.

Perhaps it was quick recognition, a glimpse of long golden streaks across its surface, a hesitation, a double take, or too much tequila, or all those things, that caused the misstep as he made his way down the side of the jetty. For whatever reason, the boulder was not as it seemed! Ever so slightly, but just enough, just as his foot touched its surface, the boulder gave way to the pressure of contact, sending Santos' foot sliding across it and jamming into a crevice. Santos fell backward, flailing his arms in frantic attempts to grab a cushion of air. He tried to hang on to the tiny key, but his hands flew open; he heard it ping against the rock just as his head smacked hard against its sharp edge.

Santos lay motionless, draped across the boulder's surface; a thick liquid trickled down its sides. Perhaps there had been mutual recognition just before contact; at any rate, as the man's life forces spilled upon him, the boulder grasped the certain knowledge: indeed, this was the same energy he had known before on the mountain and here. Talons of desperation snatched. Why had the man come here again? Had he come to take the boulder back, after all, had he sensed its true significance, and how the mountain needed him? Had he, the boulder, caused this to happen somehow?

All was still but for the man's heart weakly but incessantly pounding the weight of hours into the boulder's awareness. The night was long and empty. There was no other movement, no more humans approaching the jetty, no one searching for the injured man. Did the man, too, lack significance? Would no one ever notice he was here? And was this now to be the boulder's burden, a lifeless form across him always, blotting out the light of life, that which the boulder had soundly rejected when his? Whether or not he had caused it, the man's thumping rhythm echoed the truth of what the boulder could do to reverse it now. Nothing. Nothing. Nothing.

The eagles' boulder found himself begging once more, "Surely, this was not meant to be! It was not my intent to put an end to this man's energies! He is meant to continue!" He cried again to whatever force that had made him into the deepness of night. "Bring back this life. I meant him no harm! Let the wet, salty air come through to sting my surface again, the luster of star-shine tease at my brow! I would do anything just for that! Let the man's energies stir within him!"

The slate of night melted away into the blue-gray of a sunless dawn. Through a long, long morning, the only movement that came from the man were twitches of his little finger. "Do not let his life force leave him!" begged the boulder. Only the waves replied in monotonous crescendos of song.

It was midafternoon by the time a group of men, chattering loudly, rushed in a tight, active band toward the breakfront. They scattered and zigzagged all around back and forth, calling, "Santos! Santos, where are you? You out here?" The boulder tried to draw them to him with all the energies that remained within him. They seemed not to know he was there and ran everywhere else, all along the beach, on top of the jetty, on the other side.

It was Willie who finally stumbled upon them. "Santos! Guys! Over here!"

They all rushed in and leaned over the boulder and the man, trying to free his foot from the crevice. "He must continue!" implored the boulder. "Help him continue! Take him with you! Lift him from me!" These were both such familiar energies. They had called him Santos! Was this truly the same man that had stood so often in his presence? Were these the ones who had come to him with fish for the eagles? Had he, the eagles' boulder, caused their friend harm?"

But then, wasn't this also the man who had carried him away from his royal place on the mountain, the one who had dumped him here in this strange, wet place and left him alone?

"Santos, what are you doin' out here all by yourself, all wet and cold like this?" cried the other familiar one, leaning over the quiet man. "We slept right through breakfast, man. We thought you had too! What the heck were you doin' out here all night?"

A few of the group dashed away, then returned with others who wrapped the man's head in cloth. His heavy body was lifted slowly and eased onto a canvas bed. Finally, finally, they carried him away. None seemed to notice the old eagles' throne.

Nonetheless. Salt-sea air once again drifted unhindered onto the boulder. He opened wide his every pore and deeply sucked it in. Swooning against the warm stroking of the high sun's rays that shyly peaked at him through thick clouds, he allowed himself to experience a new awakening.

"I feel it again!" the boulder murmured in awe. "Once more, the sun warms me to the very core, nursing me with its strength, which I may preserve for all who will partake of it!" Passionately, he cried out, 'Brothers, I am ready to learn of this new existence! Teach me your song of celebration!"

A long silence stabbed at his eagerness. "It is I, the eagles' throne, prepared at last to take up my purpose beside you! Good afternoon!" he beckoned.

There was no responding salutation. Into the boulder's new vulnerability seared instead the hot tongue of rejection. "Penitence would serve you now more fittingly than celebration. It is not our purpose to cause injury to another's existence," scolded the same round boulder next to him who had chided him before.

The remorseful boulder trembled within, his excitement sinking. "But I have learned…"

"Learned what, to serve yourself? To celebrate another's pain?"

"I celebrate his continuing, and mine," the eagles' boulder cried.

"The man continues despite you," he heard back. "You continue despite yourself. You have no cause for celebration."

Furtively, the boulder discarded his new-found humility and sputtered, "Am I to blame for a man's lack of surefootedness? He might have slipped as well on any of you!"

"It was your anger that repelled him, not ours! Now you repel yourself from us with dishonesty, even as the sun bakes the energy that flowed from the man into a stain of blight upon your granite."

Stain? Horrified, the gold-flecked boulder tried to observe himself. He could see nothing. "No!" he shouted. "I am marked only by your accusations. There is no stain of guilt upon me!"

A discordant roar shot back at him. "You cannot deny it. The rejection that bled from your core now marks you without. You are not one of us!"

The eagles' boulder felt himself being shut away from the recognition of all around him. Desperate to win their acknowledgement, he begged for the waves to lick the stain, if it did exist, to wash him clean before the sun branded him ostracized forever. But the waves remained calm and aloof and seemed to deny him too, as if they feared contamination. Only the heat of the sun sought him out, glazing the stain, as he had feared, into a scar upon his existence.

When at last the wave of time began to erase the mark, the stain of denial, now of self, was etched into the boulder's being. As the pulse of universal forces continued, the rhythmic repetition of ocean waves blending and running hand in hand toward shore became to the boulder a monotonous beat, a symbolic beating for his worthlessness. Day after day, the sun rose and set, bending fused hues through the clouds and the rain, blasting its chorus of color around him. But the eagles' boulder saw less, heard less, felt less.

He was thus unaware when the rhythm changed, when all the forces of water and air took on a rushing, as if they were trying to keep frenzied pace with clouds akin to smoke that raced in like a plague, fast erasing the blue sky that retreated to safety above them. Gulls long familiar with flight unencumbered thrashed as if drowning in turbulent currents of air, smashed against invisible walls, and one by one abandoned the eager search for sustenance.

A crescendo of sound rose from the ocean and fell from the sky. All the world's forces seemed to converge into a pulsating multitude of confusion. Once-tame waves ran erratic races, angling toward uncommon goals.

From the harbor's jutting wall of rock, boulder rasps grew to whispers, shouts to cries, frantic vibrations rising in a common call: "Hold fast! We are about to be tested!"

The tension finally reached even the inert form of the long, flat boulder with golden flecks and a fading red stain. Awareness flashed upon him as waves that before only teased at his perch now drenched him completely. In the distance, a fist of darkness unclasped and reached long, skinny fingers down to earth and ocean. The rain was coming. Strong streaks of pummeling rain.

"Hold fast!" came the cry once again. Again and again, they cried out, even to the lone boulder in their midst. But the stubborn boulder's position had been weakened by his own quest for self-destruction. With each cry, he slipped a little more against the growing tumult of nature's power.

Huge waves thrashed tornadic whirls of water at the jetty. When the last great wave slashed at him, the eagles' boulder tried, earnestly, with some last shred of desire yet within him, to cling to those beneath him. But there was not enough to reach out and take hold! The big boulder was yanked from his place and washed from the jetty's side into thrashing water, tumbled about as if he were only a rock, and smashed back up against the jetty. A piece of his side was sliced away.

Finally, the boulder succumbed to the blackness that carried him out, covering him completely. There was no escape. To those on the wall and the mountain valley, the eagles' boulder would truly exist no more. What difference would it make to them, or to him anyway? What grand purpose of his would they miss or yearn for? The boulder now truly wished that so it might be, that he might simply vanish into the darkness that enveloped him, and never be again.

24

Gathering force from its own offspring, the storm billowed up and raced forward, pushing the ocean onto the sand and hurling sprawled remnants of splintered havoc everywhere, then chasing wildly after rivers of wind that skated ahead, seeking out new directions.

The she-eagle, alert with the joy of fulfilling her purpose, was this time forewarned of the threat to her world. Every quill on her body came to prickly attention. She'd been taking her turn coasting the air waves in search of a meal, but now she came to a restless stop on an open branch. Lifting her beak and her nostril skyward, she turned her head left and right, seeking all possible information. Though her belly gnawed with the pangs of hunger, she shot abruptly away from the tree and flew homeward. A great force of wind and moisture was aimed directly toward the side of the rocky hill on which she and her mate had made their home. Though protected on three sides by huge boulders, their nest was vulnerably perched on a ledge.

Soon, the sky would explode with danger. The eagle pushed harder, picking up speed.

She could have sought calm above the clouds. Instead, she aimed straight for the nest. Her mate, too, had remained true to his purpose. She found him anxiously shifting the weight of his body, searching for optimum protection for the eggs beneath him. She swooped in beside him and grasped the edge of their nest, settling her wings only half-closed, trying to balance herself. The wind increased. Bracing her back against it, she squeezed her talons shut and leaned inward to shield them both from its force. She pushed downward, shoving her beak into her breast.

Suddenly, the wind shifted to the southwest, whipping at them from an angle. Her new mate trembled, his body tense. He squeezed his talons tightly shut and opened the protective arc of his wings cautiously wider, eyeing the boulders heaped below them. If the fury continued much longer, they would have to seek refuge among them. His mate would not be easily persuaded. But the eggs would not spring forth with life if they themselves did not survive, he knew. Better survival than futile self-sacrifice. He nudged her with his beak. Weakly, she lifted her head.

He could tell she did not have the strength; it was too late for them to move safely now. He eased down into the nest so that she could squeeze in beside him. The talons of a powerful claw slipped against an exposed egg. He felt it crack and ooze beneath him. Stubbornly holding his place, he huddled against his mate's shivering body, offering her his warmth. There was no time to mourn. First, they must cling to the life that was theirs.

25

In the small hospital nearest Sand Harbor, Santos thrashed in his bed and clung to his own life. A whirlwind of sounds seemed to jab at him from distant places—a swirling brew of rain smashing against rattling windows, monotonous music and laughter without meaning, squeaking wheels of dinner carts, silver clanking against china. He could hardly separate all the sounds, barely make out shadows that bounced down the halls, shadows of nurses passing by shadows of visitors. As if through a hollow tunnel, he heard orderlies greeting patients like long-lost friends.

He could not be too hard on them. They, too, were earning their bread, playing their parts in the scheme of things, apparently oblivious to the potential that smashed at them all from outside. But Santos knew. In his most lucid, though fleeting, moments, a fresh chill would travel up and down his spine, as he reckoned with what seemed to be his new reality, though he tried and tried to reject it, to make it not so.

He knew things weren't promising when he could finally think clearly again and even Hank came to visit. "Boy, Santos, you sure know how to get outa work! First the eagles. Now this."

"Yeah, yeah, I fin' my ways," Santos teased back, more for Hank's sake than his own. "That doctor, he open his palm right up for the moneys I slip in there to make for me the big excuse."

"Yeah, well, just 'cause we've cut through the mountain, don't mean we ain't gonna need your big ol' Cuban muscles to keep goin' with the road!" chimed Willie, yanking a big handkerchief out of his back pocket to swipe at his forehead.

Santos forced a laugh. "Hah! You t'ink I don' see how shaky you get without Santos aroun' to show you what's what? You gotta wipe the sweat off your face? You don' gotta worry, Willie, I will be there to help you in no time."

A nervous ripple went around the room. No one seemed able to muster the laugh he'd been going for. They all knew it was a long shot. Dr. Flanagan had been brutally honest. "Your optic nerve took a pretty big blow," he'd said with as much sensitivity as possible. "Like I said, we're still testing. Give it some time. This could be temporary," Dr. Mueller had added, trying to buoy his spirits, "Maybe you will see a little more than you can see now someday. Maybe even more than a little. Who knows?"

Later, Santos' mind raced with the wind outside the window, *How fleeting and precious are the opportunities we hold! One careless step, and all is changed forever!*

He would not be surprised if the glass cracked inward and everyone in the hospital were suddenly carried, splashing back through it, arms flailing in a great tidal wave of change. Such was this experience of life, so unpredictable, so random and beyond one's own control really, no matter what we might think. Was there really no purpose to it at all?

Sometimes he would stare for hours into his new haze, wondering if this was his punishment for not trying harder to fulfill his purpose after God had brought him to America safely. At other times, he would wonder if there really was a God because if there was, how could He have let this happen? Had it all been Santos' imagination and rosy eyes after all?

How would he earn money now, hobbling unevenly and almost blind? Ironic. At least now, there was no difficult choice to make. He could neither destroy nor create, neither alter mountains nor build roads. Would he ever be able to paint again on canvas or velvet? Could he ever throw fish to the eagles again, given the chance?

Worst of all, would he ever be able to travel out in the boat he'd arranged for only last month, the boat to fetch Marcella and Mama' and Papa'? How would he even send for them now? He could never ask them to take care of him. What could he offer Marcella now? What would she think of him now? Would she pity him? They were expecting him to come for them soon, now that he'd sent word they'd made their way to the mountain. How would he get word to them again now? Did he even want to? Maybe he should just disappear.

"All we can really say is that we don't know how much damage has been done yet," Dr. Whitaker had added that day, still trying to make him feel better. "Like I said, they're still testing. You never really know what might happen. Don't give up hope, it's a *powerful* thing. Keep the faith."

What faith? wondered Santos. He'd only been fooling himself all those years. Okay, so even if God was the real thing. Why would He give Santos the gift and the drive, even the freedom, and then yank it all away, like snatching a spinning top from a toddler if He had something special for him to do?

It was all too much to think about. So he decided not to. Eventually, like the eagles' boulder had done, Santos began to bury his naturally hopeful heart and turned inward, toward the darkness behind his eyes. He began to think maybe he'd just as soon not live at all if it were up to him. He drifted off to sleep, taunted by visions of a brooding figure lifting its wings to float across the sunset, drop a dead rabbit by its lifeless mate, and fly away, leaving the still form mournfully behind, trapped forever in darkness. Then Santos was swimming across the jetty of boulders, solid one minute, quicksand the next, and he was frantically trying to grab on to something solid, but he kept sinking into his own black void.

26

The ball of fire spewed its first tendrils of pink into the gray sky. Calm redraped itself across the harbor, smothering slowly the storm's last breath. One lone seagull stirred timidly from his hiding place, then jumped into the sky, sounding a joyful trumpet. Emboldened brothers joined in, calling a raucous challenge to the fading roar of angry waves, revived warriors chasing the last rosy wisps of dawn as they dragged a curtain of pale blue across the horizon in their beaks.

The truth of his continued existence slid stealthily over the eagles' boulder, reminding him of the insignificance of his own will. Only a foot away from the jetty, he lay sprawled in plain view below them, entrapped by a wide swath of sand. The wall of boulders loomed over him, righteously whole. He braced himself for a chorus of taunts, defensive forces raging within. He had stood the test as well as any, even protected others below him, but his position had been too vulnerable, the storm's fury too strong!

But there were no taunts. No chants. The boulder received no recognition at all. More fully than if it truly had hammered relentlessly upon him, the boulder suffered the impact of negative force from the jetty. Perhaps his will had found its mark, after all, and he no longer existed! Now the very thing he had longed for gnawed at him with growing fear.

But gulls that had passed him by before, when he'd been but a part of the multitude, closed their wings above him and settled upon him daily, dropping their white waste over his surface. The scratching pressure of human feet increased, as he now formed a stepping stone up to the wall of boulders that seemed to leer down at him from where they belonged, still holding firm. Waves lapped hungrily at him, eating away the jagged edges of his wound. The sun seared him, breezes chilled him. If he did not exist, how could all this unpleasantness be so?

Finally, he could bear it no more and cried out, "Observe! Your brother is here, the eagles' throne, the one who was taken the night of the storm! I am wounded. You may not know me, but I am still your brother! I am not as I seem! I am more!"

Only echoes of his own vibrations returned to the boulder. Every echo, every cry, every new wave that washed upon him, then ventured back out to its own, drained a bit more the energy that had peaked anew within him since the night of the storm. Waves merged into tides. The eagles' boulder again yielded to the cover of darkness. There was no more reason for wishing, and fear would change nothing but his private battle. He began to expect that his fate was simply to endure until the forces were done with him and had worn him down enough to carry him out to sea for the rest of his continuing, there tumbling him in the constant blackness down to true nonexistence. So be it. He only mourned everything in between.

27

In the valley, mourning had waned in the slow, wide wake of the storm. The female eagle had endured, as had all her eggs, except the one whose life had slipped from its shell during the high winds. Now warmth fluttered its oncoming promise beneath her. She let out a trumpet blare into the open ear of the heavens, "Aaaaeeee!" Shifting, she searched the distance; so far, only scattered wisps of white floated across empty skies. Suddenly, a faint picking beneath her mushroomed into sharp cracks.

The blossoming mother sang out loudly with her own sharp sound, "Eeeeaaaah" A far-off reply mingled with the sudden chirp within the nest. The first shell had collapsed beneath the eager spark of new life! "Eeeeaah!"

A small shadow took form and shot toward her, growing rapidly larger, closer until a massive umbrella of wings blotted out all else and descended to the nest. Closing his wings, the male eagle cocked his head, eyeing the bristling movements. A tiny cloud stretched an open beak toward him, then fell over. The male parent reached down and nuzzled the first newborn with his own beak. Beside it, another egg rocked within the cradle of the nest. The female's fidgeting increased. A jagged crack formed on the egg, and life burst forth from its confines, another puff of downy white.

The pain of loss softened into a haze of poignant memory. Life was indeed for the living! It was good to be completely embroiled in the joy of fulfilling the purpose that was hers.

Occasionally, her mind's eye had replayed fondly those days in the valley with her first family, of Wings as he'd clung to the long, flat surface, of watching him learn to soar proudly next to her. She often wondered if he had found others like them at the place by the great waters, *Would she see him again, maybe even his own offspring someday? Would they ever return to the place of their beginning, where his young could...*

"Eeeeaaah!" The new father interrupted her imaginings, as he pushed off from the nest in search of sustenance befitting a first meal for their offspring. Quickly, he circled around and aimed back toward them. The timeless dreams of sporadic journeys led by the heart-pound of impulse drifted now into a swooning loop of the proud bird that was now her mate. The strong, sure stroke of his wings was bringing him back to fulfill her needs and the needs of their new ones in the nest. Old memories faded. A comforting warmth emanated from her breast. "Eeeeeeee!" she called. "We await your return! We will be here!"

28

S o, too, as the season of storms passed, ocean spray
that had long chilled the eagles' boulder to the core
misted his surface with increasing warmth. Humans
trudged past him, hoisting smaller boulders, heaving them
onto the sand nearby to form low circles of granite. As they
gathered around them, humming a tumult of shared joy,
orange flames licked the salt air with vibrancy. Night after
night, hot sparks danced like fireflies through the night,
caressing and teasing the lone boulder on the sand by
the jetty.

All along the wide stretch of beach, circles of boulders,
humans and flames worshiped their existence together,
permeating the salty air with pungent aroma, laughter
and music. For many nights, the eagles' boulder only
observed, resisting the urge to open his pores once more
to the vulnerability of longing for change. Nevertheless,
a stubborn trickle of caring began to well up from deep
within. He tried to squelch his rising desire to feel the hot

glow drying his dampness, to absorb the touch of other boulders in shared purpose and celebration. Change had wrought him thus far only violence and decline; he dared not wish for it again! Even if he did, who or what would heed the wish of one so ignored before?

At any rate, the humans always passed him by, gathered nearby, even used him as a stepping stone to hike onto the breakfront, without taking note of his presence. He had no intention of emanating a plea on the night when three men came toward him just after sunset. "Looks like all the fire rings are already taken," one of the men announced.

Despite self-warning, the eagles' throne could not help but try to emit, "Gather here! I am as good as any other to fill your needs!"

To his astonishment, one of them stopped beside him. "Here's a big one to start with," he suggested. "Why don't we just look for a couple more to carry over here, and we'll be ready to roast? My stomach's growlin'!"

"Don't you think we might get wet? This thing's awful close to the water."

"Think we could push it up a couple feet? The tide shouldn't come that far up."

Three sets of hands reached underneath the long, flat boulder and pulled up against him. Despite self-warning, he began to envision a new place, wings and freedom, significance in the scheme of things, warmth and sharing. But the eagles' boulder budged not a fathom. Breathless, the men fell back onto the sand. "You gotta be kiddin'!" gasped one of the men. "I can press one hundred pounds, how about you?"

"Come on, we can do it!" said the one who'd first been drawn to the boulder. "Let's go get George and Les! What's keepin' 'em anyway? And Ken, I know he's been to the gym lately."

Now it was becoming a game. For a short while, they retreated together up the slope. There was brash laughter, distant, then quickly closer and louder, along with the whomping disturbance of running feet across the beach toward the eagles' boulder. "What's the matter, didn't you take your vitamins this morning?" said a new voice.

The boulder trembled imperceptibly, hope rising and falling within him like the ocean waves, as six sets of hands reached beneath and exerted combined pressure against his surface. The eagles' boulder budged not at all.

"That thing's heavier than it looks!" said the first man, giving up.

"Yeah, I didn't come to the beach to work anyway, or break my back over a stupid rock."

The boulder heard a low chuckle. The men trudged away, huffing and puffing, leaning on each other. "There must be some smaller ones closer to where we wanta be."

"Closer wouldn't hurt. Boy, I thought all that working out would pay off a little better! That thing made me feel like the beach weakling!"

The laughter of the six friends waned with their footsteps. The boulder was left with familiar aloneness, now joined by the turmoil of confusion. Was he simply a toy of the universe created for fate's entertainment? Why had he felt so weighted down, no matter how he had struggled? Yet, during the storm, he'd been light enough to be tossed about like a pebble!

Anger broiled across his confusion. In a blast of pent-up frustration, he clenched his innermost self into a ball as futilely threatening as a man's fist raised against heaven and tried to scream, "Stop playing with me!"

"So who's playing?" squeaked a tiny voice.

Shocked, the boulder followed the thin trail of vibrations. A small rock, dull and gray, its knobby shape scattered with pockmarks, piped, "Anyway, what if I *were* playing? Do you dislike humor?"

"I do when I'm at the brunt of it," growled the boulder. "Do you like being so small you can sneak up and invade another's place? When did you get here anyway? Where did you come from?"

"Most recently, from the vast world of wetness out there. Fascinating world, quite different from here. As to when, just now, when a friendly wave rendered me right to this spot beside you. Fine spot. Fine ride. Fine wave too, gentle, smooth. Fine day, isn't it? Haven't felt the sun for quite a spell. What have you got to be so grumpy about?"

"What have you got to be so giddy about?" the boulder shot back, studying him skeptically.

The rock responded lightly, "Just being, I suppose. Resting on this fine beach, these tender grains of sand. Soothing to the granite, aren't they?"

"This sand has helped to wear you down to the pitiful shape you're in, just as it wears at me even now. I see nothing tender in that."

"Pitiful? I, pitiful?" The rock sighed. "Small boulder, take note. I am all that I am. I have been all that I was. And I am yet to be everything that I will be. What's to be pitied in that?"

"I suppose your existence has been less trying than mine," said the boulder. "But you are right. Your near-nonexistence is to be envied more than pitied. But why do you call me small? I am more than one hundred of you."

"And less than one of you," said the rock, sighing again. "You have not heard me at all. I can see why the fates have dropped me here, and what is to be the purpose of my energies on this beach."

"A noble purpose, no doubt," snickered the boulder. "What is it about granite that strives so for nobility and purpose?"

"All of existence," said the rock, "in striving for its true purpose, achieves its nobility."

"Well, this existence strived for purpose and achieved defeat. And what do you mean, 'I'm less than one of me?' Why do you talk such nonsense?"

"Your defeat is your lack of acceptance. Simply allow yourself to be all that you are, wherever you are at any given moment, and you will find the victory of your true purpose as it is meant to be. Stop fighting yourself and the forces that shape you and your purpose. It's as simple as that! I don't talk nonsense. You hear nonsense."

"Well, whatever it is, I don't care to absorb what you emote."

"Fine. Fine with me, fine and dandy. I have no intention of forcing that which you are not ready to absorb. An impossible feat at any rate, you know."

"Nonsense again. I doubt I shall ever be ready for your nonsense. Leave me alone."

"I shall leave you alone. However, I cannot leave you. You are aware of that, are you not? That is not a matter of choice. Aloneness is."

"Nonsense. I have been alone against my will. Now I choose to be alone, and I cannot. I have no choices at all."

The rock offered no answer. A shield of silence raised itself between the two granite bodies. The boulder tried to ignore the quick heaviness of its impact. Night moved in, dropping a shroud of fog that seemed to erase the small rock from existence altogether. The larger rock sought the refuge of relief but found, instead, a simmering regret. Perhaps he should not have directed the acid of his own anger toward one so disfigured—but the rock was so self-righteous he seemed not even to recognize his own handicap! And why did he accuse the boulder of being less than himself? What a strange thing to say—double-talk not worth trying to understand. Meaningless thoughts. A useless attempt to fill the emptiness.

A sudden chill moved across the boulder's surface. Perhaps the boulder had wrought the small rock out of the air to fill his own emptiness! Perhaps the rock did not exist at all!

"Why do you doubt in the darkness what you have known in the light?" a small voice beckoned beside him.

Stunned, the boulder didn't try to answer. Had he wrought a voice from the void now?

"You have wrought your own isolation and defeat. You have not wrought me or that which I express to you."

"Well, wherever you came from, how is it that our communication always begins with your invasion of my private thoughts?" the boulder sputtered defensively. "I did not call out to you!"

"Your thoughts were darting through the darkness, searching rather frantically for me, I observed. They were in need of an answer."

"I need nothing from you. My thoughts need nothing from you. Leave me and my thoughts alone."

"Your choice. Your thoughts are your own."

"Then why do you keep invading them?"

"Why do they keep calling out?"

"They don't!"

"Yes, they do."

"What do I have to do, shut off all vibrations emanating from my existence? Is that the only way to escape your presence?"

There was no reply. The boulder waited with expectation but heard nothing more than the sounds of the ocean. He tried to retreat from reckoning with the reality of a small rock which seemingly could reach beyond the boundaries of reality itself. Did the little rock truly exist? Why would the boulder conjure one so quick to try his own patience, when his confusion was already great? He had no use for one who made it worse with riddles. He would rather be alone unto himself. Safe.

"You have wrought your own isolation and defeat," the rock had declared.

Indeed, nothing could be further from the truth. He had not destroyed his own mountain nor dragged himself away from it. Neither had he created the storm that had wrenched him from the wall and dropped him into this sandy pit of aloneness.

"Your choice," the rock had said.

His choice. How could that be? What choice did he have? How could he move himself, or be something other than what he was? The mountain had been changed forever. He would never again be a significant part of its greatness. The eagles no longer needed him, having opened their wings so easily to find the purpose that was theirs in another place, far away from the boulder that had served so loyally as their throne. What purpose could he find to fulfill here, stuck on the sand, other than sit here throughout all the days and nights of his time, to be splashed and stepped on and dropped on by others?

All through the darkness he pondered, despite his resolve. Perhaps, at least, he did have some choice now, small and insignificant though it might be. At least, he did not have to be completely alone. If the rock was truly to be a part of his reality now, their destinies intermingled, their fates intertwined, perhaps he might indulge him with a bit of pleasant chatter. No debates, no deep involvement, only a touch of sharing to fill the emptiness of their time. The time of existence was not much longer for the little rock after all—if he really did exist.

As soon as dawn began to strip the mask of night, the boulder checked the spot beside him where the rock had been. There it was, knobby, full of holes, its blight of dullness manifesting the impossibility of any power to overcome the bindings of his reality.

"Look, little rock," he said gently. "I'd like to apologize…"

"One who finds it necessary to apologize to others owes the apology first to himself," announced the rock.

"Look, no more double-talk, all right? Can't we just be friends?"

"Ah, but I *am* your friend," replied the rock. "And have been all along."

"Good, then no more double-talk, all right?"

"But I am first a friend to myself and, therefore, readily able to be your friend. You, on the other hand, are not your own friend and, therefore, not mine."

"Look, I don't understand a thing you've said," retorted the boulder, anger flashing. "All I understand about you is what I behold before me. I don't mean to be cruel, little rock, but I see you as less than I. And I'm not much."

"You don't see me any more fully than you see yourself," replied the rock with irritating calm. "And that is why you are less. I am not more. You are simply less."

"You, little rock, are all mixed up. Actually, I'm *more* than I am, if anything. Not long ago, six men tried to move me and—"

"Yes, I know," the rock interjected.

"What do you mean, 'you know'? How do you know?"

The rock continued, "I'm not talking about being weighted down with yourself," he said. "As a matter of fact, that's the trouble! Why not stop fighting with the weight of your defiance and allow yourself to become all that you are meant to be? Don't you see, small boulder, you are here and now! At every moment, you…are."

"I am," said the boulder. "Okay, that's easy. I am. You really like this nonsense game, don't you? But I'm not fighting anyone except you because you're the only other one here."

"You are fighting yourself. By defying the forces that shape your existence, you are not only fighting that which you are at any given moment. You prevent that which you are meant to become."

"The forces! Ah, the forces! Are you daft? All I can do is try to protect myself from those forces!" the boulder retorted. "I've seen what they've had in store for me. Long ago, I stopped pleading with them. And you, little rock, what have they done for you? I hate to keep harping on this, but if you'd study your reflection in the water..."

"I know what I am," said the rock. "Perhaps by your standards, I am small and lacking in beauty. But I am not insignificant. One never knows how one's existence might affect the existence of another at any given moment as we are meant to do—as I am affecting yours right now and as you affect others as well. Small boulder, you do have a choice. Though you in the moments and the moments in you may seem mundane or trivial, the effect of your own significance reverberates forever. As it is meant to do."

"Yeah, sure," said the boulder. "I am here to make a significant squatting stone for every passing gull. And not long ago, I proved my significance to a poor adventurer..."

"The man's injury was proof of your significance upon events of the world outside yourself. Exactly my point," said the rock. "And also proof of the insignificance of the world within you."

"I thought you had been in the world of wetness. How do you know all these things that have happened to me?"

The small rock did not reply.

"There is no world within me, only granite" continued the boulder. "What are you talking about? I don't understand a thing you are saying!"

"Yes, you do," said the rock. "Understanding is yours. Simply open up to it."

"I don't know what to open up to! I'm a boulder, little rock, hard, misshapen now, since I tumbled from the wall. I am wingless, legless. What would you have me open up to? And how?"

A shadow sliced between them. The boulder's awareness cringed from the sudden presence of a small girl who had slipped up beside him and placed a feather-like hand on his surface.

"Look, Mommie!" she called, removing her hand from him and bending down toward the smaller rock.

"No!" cried the boulder.

But already, the rock was in the child's hand. "What are all those sparkly things?" she asked.

A larger shadow intermingled with the first and fell across the boulder. "Just part of the rock, honey, minerals, things that have gathered together to make it what it is. It looks pretty in the sun, doesn't it?"

"He is dull!" cried the boulder. "Put him back where he belongs, find a pretty one!"

"Uh-huh," murmered the girl. "Like it's got lots of little stars in it. Mommie, look how it fits just right in my hand! See, it's exactly the same as this part. Isn't that funny? Like it was made just for me?"

"That's your palm. It is a good fit."

The girl closed her fingers over the rock. "I want to take it home! Can I, Mommie?"

"No! Put him back!" the boulder screamed from his innermost core, surprising himself. "He will mean nothing to you! He belongs here on the beach with those of his kind, not shut away with humans! Little rock, do something! You can break the chains of reality! Break free!"

"I am free," said the rock. "As are you!"

"I'll keep it on my windowsill, where the light can help it show off its shine," the girl babbled happily. "Water wears it down, doesn't it, Mommie? I'm gonna keep it safe with me all the way 'til I'm grown up. Then I can give it to my little girl. Or boy! It could just go on and on like our pictures, couldn't it? Do you think this rock could go on forever, Mommie?

The shadows began to move away. Every part of the boulder reached out, trying in vain to stop them. "He's my friend!" he moaned. "Please, don't take away my friend!"

"Now you must be a friend to yourself," the little rock called back, his voice marking a diminishing trail that followed the human's footprints through the sand.

29

They walked directly toward a tall man who moved a cane back and forth like a snake testing its environment as he approached. He could barely see them, but he didn't wonder who they were, or if they knew him. They passed him by, moving around him, careful not to startle him or get in his way. The little girl hushed her chatter and looked at him sadly.

Santos was alone now. He felt his life had been lost along with the precious mailbox key the night of his fall. He had refused more than once the efforts of his friends to have another key made in his behalf. He couldn't bear having them read Marcella's letters to him or not knowing how to answer her. And so he'd decided his life would belong to no one. His buddies said he wasn't trying very hard, and that wasn't like him.

He knew they were right. That's why he'd made his way here with a fresh piece of canvas and the new set of oils the nurses had foisted upon him. He did have a picture in his mind, a brilliant sunset laying a path across the water, sort of a gold carpet for Marcella from Cuba to America, an easier path than he had taken.

His heart softened at the thought of Marcella and his mama' and papa'. Was it more cruel for him to leave them hanging, wondering where he was, how he was, or to tell them the truth and good-bye, perhaps forever? He didn't know, and so he decided to do nothing, at least for now, until he could figure something out, or things got better— or until he learned they would never get better, that he would never regain his sight at all. He shuddered at the thought of that possibility, which seemed all too probable.

Leaning against a latticed bank not far from the jetty where he'd been injured, Santos propped a board over his lap with the canvas on top. Though he stared out toward the horizon, most of what he planned to paint would have to be stirred up from memory. He was hoping if he waited long enough he might get enough of a glimpse for the inspiration to start and carry the magic down to his hands, as it used to do. But sitting there, waiting in the noisy quiet, he saw again shadowy visions of the lone, brooding she-eagle mourning the loss of her mate. *Would Marcella mourn like that when she heard of his condition?*

Always in the back of his mind, Santos wondered how the two eagles were doing, if the young one had ever forgotten the flying fish of his first days, and if they'd claimed a new territory. He was afraid they would never find a place to match the grandeur of the home they were forced to leave so abruptly. Someday he would try to recall enough details to bring it all to life on canvas—the eagles, their boulder, the mountain—the balanced majestic perfection of the whole valley.

At least now, he could relate more to the shock they must have felt, stripped so suddenly of all they had known. And he could no longer say he did not have the time to create. He just couldn't get inspired anymore. Now just being was challenge enough.

All through lunch and late afternoon, he sat, his mind busy, but his fingers idle. Though life still danced in brilliant colors across his mind, he didn't dare try to reproduce it with colors and marks he couldn't see. The top of his head began to sweat heavily under the broad-rimmed straw field hat. Just before sunset, he reached for his cane, pushed himself up, and stepped stiffly away, carrying the blank canvas under his free arm.

30

He'd had no idea that the boulder, which had so significantly affected his life, was near and had known of his presence. Nor that the boulder mourned his leaving the same as it had with the sudden departure of the small rock, carried so abruptly away right in the middle of their curious talk.

Soon, all was quiet again. Only the waves whispered, whooshed, whispered, whooshed, "Forever, forever, forever, forever! Forever, forever, forever, forever!" Sprinkling the boulder with their mist, they sent forth a haze up, up, and gathered into white puffs high above, waiting. The truth of their song floated its fullness into the air. Time stood hushed and unmoving, yet ran shouting into forever. All was constant, yet changing; new, yet old, beginning and ending in the whisk of each moment. Everything seemed to stand alone. Yet everything was forever entwined.

As night erased the misted blue and crawled toward the boulder shyly, the boulder began to sift the whys and wherefores of his past through the sieve of his struggling. Had he truly never yet been all? He was bound by the limitations of his existence. To be more seemed impossible. How, without wings, or even arms, was he to open himself, as the rock had advised? And to what? How was he fighting himself? How could he alter the decisions of fate and their effects on him? Obviously, his will had no power against the fates. Against. No power against. Hmmmmm.

"By fighting the very forces that shape you, you are fighting yourself," the strange little rock had said. *Is that what he had meant?*

Night enveloped the town of Sand Harbor. As the forces flung stars one by one across a black velvet sky, the boulder pondered the rock's words and felt the burgeoning gleam of knowledge slowly, then swiftly, waking within him. Where their first separate utterance had left him confused, their joined impact now began to enlighten him. Though physically unaltered, he knew he would never again be the same. The apparently insignificant little ball of granite had left its impression on him just as on the sand where he'd lain and under the water that had washed upon him and now swept his traces away—but whose energies would forever be altered just because he had been there.

Before the night was done, though understanding was far from complete, the eagles' boulder vowed, at least, that his own fight was finished. He had no idea how to become more; he had no magic powers to change, no wings or legs to move himself to another place. All he could do was be what he was, where he was. That would be his purpose for now. He knew, at least, from the coming and passing of the little rock, that this sand, this beach, and all the ocean would not be as they were and would be without him and those like him.

When the rosebud of morning unfolded around him, he timidly opened himself to it. To all the forces, he opened up as best he could, imploring them to leave a part of themselves with him. In time, perhaps the vacuum of his world within would be filled, and he would no longer be less than he could be. If, indeed, he was less. He could only gamble on the rock's truth. But even if the rock were wrong, his satisfaction seemed truth enough. Better, at least, than what had been his own misery.

31

The boulder was not alone in his growth. All across the hemisphere, growth of another kind was running rampant. Spring had multiplied the earth's families near to the ocean and far. The lofty mother eagle was once again responsible for three destinies more than her own. As all her ancestors before her had done, though in a different place, she knew instinctively that she must track faithfully the path of parental constancy, serving beside her mate a steady feast of nagging and nourishing. She had done well by her destiny. She had answered the call of her purpose. Now she marveled at the resplendent response of her offspring as they nearly burst the sides of the nest. Soon it would be time to display for them the strength and quickness and courage required in survival's flight, as it seemed she had learned herself such a short time ago. Often, she searched the distance instinctively, expecting to see the one she had first taught to come gliding toward her as he had so many times before.

She could not have known that just being had become a struggle for the young one she searched for. So briefly, he had allowed himself to be diverted away from the purpose that was his. Now weakened, he reckoned with a plight he had not known before— how to get where he wanted, needed, had to go. He must find his way to others like himself soon; he must make his way to Eagle Island. Probably, it was already too late to find his mother again. He wondered if she and her new mate were flying now, off in search of a convocation moving south. Perhaps they had already joined one.

He didn't know how long she'd been gone from his side. He was only aware that the days and nights had fled from him in a streak of confusion since first he'd lost his strong concentration, surrendering only momentarily to the pull of the unfamiliar, the tantalizing tug of a warm stream of air, a harmlessly fleeting pause. He'd fought with shocked fury to escape when it suddenly gathered strength, sucking him toward its center with the powerful vacuum of currents at war. But by then, the sky had held foreboding might, with bulging fists of clouds thrusting into oblivion all the rhythms of reason so long dependable and taken for granted! Like a giant beater, the storm had whipped him into its frothing eye and whisked him along its mad way.

A lesser bird, or one less determined, would not have survived at all. When the storm had finally finished with him, having drawn his energy into its own, it had dumped him with casual abandon onto strange ground. He had floundered, trying to regain his sense of direction ever since—but his bearings were lost and confused! Which was the way to the valley's rock edging out of these thick, tall pines? Weren't these the same trees he'd fallen through, crashing from branch to branch down to the ground so many days before?

His right wing shouted with pain. Again and again, he had struggled to reach a low branch from which to launch his flight back to freedom. He had not made it yet; his strength was waning. But he would try again, until he had finally worked his way out of these towering masses that cruelly encroached upon his very existence. Surely, when he did manage to reach a clearing, his senses would not fail him; he would then be able to discern which direction to go. He would win, as he had always won, conquer this new threat to his greatness, fly with one wing, if necessary. If only this dampness that clung to his feathers did not make him feel so uncommonly heavy!

32

Not far away, on the beach of Sand Harbor, the eagle's old friend, the boulder, was still heavy with dampness as well. He was often doused by mischievous waves, at times even completely covered by the waters of the high tides. The surprise was in the pleasure! Never before had the day seemed so bright, the sun so warming, the breeze so gently nudging him into further wakefulness! The bustle of life teemed all around him: frail-legged birds skating about in a frenzy of pecking; rubbery plants lying by the shore languidly like boys on a board, waiting to catch a rushing wave; a bulky mirage of a turtle emerging from the sea and lumbering like a boulder with legs up and beyond him to dig in the sand and then return once more to the sea. Had all this been here before and he just hadn't seen it or felt it? His pleasure grew to eagerness as days opened and closed before him. Soon, even the touch of the gulls on his back tickled more than scratched; a soaring within his own existence replaced his longing for their wings.

His former resentment of lapping waves was now a source of constant amusement, both from the touch and the vision. He developed a game of silently cheering separate bits of swathing foam that crowded into hurried throngs in childlike races to reach him first and swirl about his base, depositing sand, then sweeping it clean. Done, they gathered themselves into groups of bubbles and skimmed in file like obedient ducklings back out to sea. He never knew what to expect. Sometimes the waves stayed far away, close to their main body, avoiding him like a plague; others crept up to him slowly, teased all around him caressingly, then lazed away; some rushed upon him unawares, brushing his crown with brief submersion; at other times, the submersion was full, and always seemingly but never really final. He plunged himself into each contact, his surrender complete and, therefore, painless.

There was no small rock to offer encouragement or even to pass the time of day, no call of acceptance from the wall. But human lovers now often spread their blankets before him and leaned against him, unaware that in so doing, they were sharing with a big piece of granite the fullness of their joyful energies. Children who once ignored the boulder's presence now climbed on him, hid playfully from each other behind him, and dug side by side in the sand next to him, their exuberant celebration of life emanating from them into the boulder's fully opened pores.

One day in early spring, a little girl dragged her feet sullenly through the sand, creating a long track across the beach. She stopped in front of the boulder and rubbed her tiny hands across his granite.

"Becky?"

The girl turned her body slowly in the direction of the woman's voice but gave no reply. Leaning into the boulder's warmth, she backed into its old wound and lowered her body against it to the bottom, where the granite formed a narrow ledge just above the sand. The fit was perfect, and she nestled in, apparently comforted.

Her Aunt Julie placed her beach chair at a respectable distance and sat down, relieved for the moment from this uncommon worry. *Whatever works*, she thought, wondering how they would get through the summer. With no children of her own, she had plenty of time; offering Becky refuge while her parents recovered from the accident seemed the natural thing to do. "It'll be fun for me. We can play house!" she'd offered glibly. "She'll love the beach. I'll take her every day."

But Becky had lost her outgoing spirit; she didn't seem to love anything or anybody. She'd hardly spoken, muttered only required responses for almost two weeks, and seemed to be withdrawing more every day. Should she tell her brother his daughter seemed more traumatized by the accident than any of them had realized? Right now, their energies were concentrated on trying to get back to as near normalcy as possible—the last thing they needed to hear was that Becky wasn't thriving in this awesome environment.

Julie felt uncommonly helpless, not wanting to let her niece down, but not knowing how to reach her. She was tempted to call Becky closer, demand she get exercise, have some fun; but something within commanded otherwise. Her limp little body was slumped listlessly against the big boulder. In the sun's glare, she appeared almost melded to it, one with the rock. For some unknown reason, her aunt discerned that, for the moment, at least, Becky was right where she belonged, in her own element for the first time since arriving.

Always open to small miracles, Julie smiled and turned her attention toward the waves. For the rest of the afternoon, she studied the constant motion and change, change she had always thought was so much more predictable than life. Now, for the first time, she marveled at the uniqueness of every wave, the subtle distinctiveness of the design each wave left on the sand as it retreated back out to sea. Funny, she'd never noticed that before.

The chill of evening had already moved in by the time the girl reluctantly allowed herself to be drawn from the boulder. All through the night, the essence of a familiar warmth remained within the boulder's existence. The next morning, it felt so grand again, opening his pores to collect the sun's heat as much as he could, just as he had for the eagles. He would hold it close and save it for the child in case she returned!

And so she did, that afternoon, in silent ritual, trudging toward the long, low slab of granite, leaning against it, sitting alone on the bottom ledge, absorbing the boulder's warmth, unaware she was sharing with him, as well. Day after day, they came, her aunt sitting nearby, occasionally beckoning her niece toward another child, still wanting to believe that playing was more normal and thus more desirable than sitting.

But Becky, though small, seemed to know what she needed at these moments in her time; she clung to the boulder's solidity as if she truly had become part of him, and he of her. The gold-flecked granite, once throne to powerful eagles, now proudly served a dainty princess.

And that is what popped out of her one day, quite unexpectedly, as a girl near her age walked by.

"I am a princess, you know!" Becky called out.

"You are?" replied the girl, looking doubtful. " From what country?"

Her aunt watched in astonishment, her eyes welling with tears as Becky produced from her lunch bag the windmill cookies she'd begged for that morning. Like a trophy, she held one up and sang out, "From Denmark! Would you care for a cookie from my country?"

The other girl's body was tanned like copper, the top of her head a tousled coil of gold. She hesitated only a moment, then spun and ran toward the water, where she leaned down quickly, plucked a small perfect shell from the sand and held it out to Becky as she raced back to her.

"Welcome to my island! May I share your throne, princess? What is your name?"

Her vibrant being shouting abundance, she worked her toes through the sand right up to Becky and her

171

boulder, then turned around and nuzzled her back into the indentation beside her, content to sit on the sand in her trench. "I think this throne was made just for us!" she announced, taking a bite out of the cookie as she offered the shell to Becky. Smiling broadly, Becky agreed.

Thus began a delicious affair that lasted all through the summer; each day, the girls were drawn to the boulder, abandoning themselves as children do to the simple relishing of life, little knowing they gave in receiving. The boulder absorbed their vibrations of joy and purred within like a cat being stroked, as they partook of the warmth the sun's rays had given to him and built their lives of fantasy and fact around him. Wisely now, Julie watched from her chair, still at a distance, marveling at the restoration of Becky's spirit. One day, it seemed her niece would never be happy again; the next, it seemed she had never been sad. Somehow, both she and her niece had grown that summer. Never before had she felt so aware! And the eagles' boulder had never felt more fulfilled of his purpose, even on the mountain.

But one windy morning, when the world at Sand Harbor turned suddenly chilly, as it was meant to do, Becky approached the boulder alone, moving slowly, feet dragging once more. Patting its granite with unbridled ceremony, she placed her lips against it and whispered, "I wish I could stay here forever, or take you with me, along with the whole ocean and all the sand, and my other friend too!"

Then she giggled. "But I can't! I gotta go back home to Mommy and Daddy!" and ran, high-kicking heels spraying sand behind her as she reached up to clasp her aunt's hand and skipped beside her toward a waiting car.

The boulder knew she would not return. The loss was painful, too sudden, as always. For a long while, he wanted to fight, give in to the dirge of self-pity. But sadness could be celebrated if met with the goal of acceptance. This too he had learned since his encounter with the small rock. He would always hold the joy of their sharing within him. It would become a part of him, even as was the pain of their loss.

Resolutely, the boulder turned his attention toward the scalloping traces of waves that chased on the sand after those that left them and then were swept up in the new design. Such was the way things were and would be. He had chosen to be fully a part of all things. He didn't know yet if he was all he was meant to be. He only knew that he was growing, even as his granite was slowly being worn away.

33

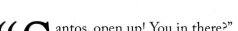

"Santos, open up! You in there?"

Startled awake, Santos flung the lumpy pillow off his head, rolled over and leaped out of bed, fists clenched, ready to fight. It wasn't until his bare feet hit the cold linoleum that he remembered he had to move cautiously now, shuffle carefully, one slow step at a time. The truth slammed into his chest worse than any fist. Doubling over, he fell back onto the rumpled bed and felt around for the pillow to hide under it again.

The other fist was knocking harder on the door now, more demanding. "Santos, wake up! It's Willie!"

"Go away, I'm asleep!"

Santos heard Willie laughing. "Yeah, well you coulda fooled me! Come on, it's time to get up and out! The sun's way up there already!"

"Yeah? Well, you coulda fooled me!" Santos flung back, not even trying to resist the urge.

Willie stopped knocking. Santos heard him sigh. The door cut a swath of silence between them now, but Santos could feel Willie's disappointment. Suddenly panicked, he tensed for the sound of footsteps going back down the stairs; he had learned Willie wouldn't tolerate much self-pity. He sprang back up and bolted to the door in three big steps, taking his chances. His left hand working the latch and the knob, he opened the door with his right hand already extended, a guilty slant of a grin on his unshaven face.

"Good gawd, man, you look awful!" Willie growled, capturing his hand and shaking his whole arm as if it were a pump, and somewhere down there, he knew there was water.

"Oh yes? Well, you look worse, I am sure of that!" jibed Santos. "I am just glad I no longer have to see so good that ugly face on your head!"

"Yeah, yeah, you should be so ugly," said Willie. His voice softened as he added, "But it sure is good to see you, anyway. I miss you out there, Santos. The whole gang does." Pushing past him into the room, he joked, "If you weren't standin' there in your shorts, I'd give you a hug, I'm so glad to see you!"

Santos felt his face redden as he laughed and turned to fumble around for his pants on the chair by the bed and put them on, zipping them up as he made his way toward the stove in the corner. "You want to get really awake? How about a cup of well-seasoned Cuban coffee, warmed three times to bring out its stoutest flavor and richest aroma?"

Willie chuckled obligingly. "Naw, I'll pass. Let's go get some weak stuff down at the diner. You and me, we have to talk."

"Sounds heavy. Go ahead, start talkin', don' just stan' there." Squinting in the direction of Willie's voice, he made out his shadow and quickly corrected himself, "Or sit there either."

"Very good, my friend, you're gettin' a handle on it. But talk will follow food!" Grabbing Santos' jacket, he placed his hand square in the middle of his friend's back, as Santos had so often done to him, and shoved him firmly toward the door.

It wasn't until after they'd both stuffed themselves with the steak and egg special and were somewhere around their third cup of real coffee that Willie reached into his back pocket and pulled out a carefully folded envelope. With no introduction or request, he began to read:

> My Dear Santos:
>
> It is with a sad and fearful heart that I shout across the seas once more. I pray this time you will reach back, assuring those who love you here that you are all right, and that you still care for us, and our welfare..."

Santos pushed his chair back and jumped up, clasping the edge of the table for support, the veins on his neck and forehead swelling. "Where did you get this?" he demanded. "You ask no permission. How do you get what is meant for me, Santos? Now I have lost all freedom, the very thing I come to America for!" His voice grew louder, oblivious to the shocked hush of everyone else in the diner. "And you read this aloud to me and to everyone here without asking me, is it okay, Santos, would it be all right? In Cuba, such rudeness would not be tolerated! How did you do this, Willie? How long have you had my key and not tol' me?"

Willie responded guiltily, surprised at his friend's reaction, "Just today, Santos. I wanted to surprise you. The post office had another key made for you."

But he wasn't deterred. Biting his tongue against scolding or offering even a hint of advice, he sucked in his breath, held it a minute, and continued reading aloud,

> "...I beg you, Santos, if not for me—if you are well and have chosen another—simply get word to your mama' and papa'—at least give us some signal through those we know and trust. We hear that Manuel's papa is in the big camp, as we feared. They say he is gravely ill, his spirit broken. It is too late now for Manuel to come to his aid despite his success in America. Your mama' weeps often. Your papa' remains stoic but more silent each day. Please, if you can, give them at least cause for encouragement; let them know somehow that you are okay. Help them to keep their spirits alive! Always they will need you. For now, I do as well. But after this letter,

I will not say again that I love you though, of course,
I do and will always. As ever, Marcella.

Santos was still standing, his head bowed prayer-like
when Willie finished. Lowering himself to the chair, he
leaned back, not bothering to pull it back close to the
table. One tear escaped and rolled brazenly down his
embarrassed cheek.

Softly, Willie answered the unasked question, "The guy
at the post office heard what happened to you. He's been
savin' your mail. I took the liberty of openin' this one since it
smells like perfume, and I thought you'd want to hear from
her whether you know it or not."

Santos didn't move or speak. People around them
finished their meals, shoved chairs around, talked in low
voices, shuffled in and out of the door, clanked silver against
china. If he hadn't known better, Santos could have sworn
he was back in the hospital. He almost longed for its subtle
deception of security, its perfectly acceptable retreat from
demands and expectations.

"If you can't write it yourself, you can dictate it to me,"
Willie pressed lightly, breaking the silence. "I always wanted
to try my hand at bein' a secretary. I'll even mail it for you."

"No! You must promise me, no matter what happens,
you will never mail anything to them from here. Look
for yourself. This letter was mailed in America beyond
prying eyes."

"Miami!" Willie proclaimed, surprised. "I didn't even notice, but how'd it get there?"

"Through those we know and trust, just as I got here."

"Well then, you must know how to do it, buddy. Tell me what I can do to let them know you're okay without puttin' anyone in jeopardy."

"Okay? That is a very little word for such a big meaning," snapped Santos. "How do we put into words, 'Santos is okay, except that God took back the gift that He gave, because He was only teasing, or we were just dreaming, and Santos can barely see, therefore he cannot work to earn money. He cannot paint or draw to fulfill everyone's hopes and dreams, he is less than the man you fell in love with, he has even lost the freedom he came to America for and, therefore, so sorry he cannot send for those he loves. But do not fear. Now that Santos is unable to become an artist of value to the party, perhaps his escape from the homeland will be insignificant and now will put no one in *jeopardy!*'"

He stood abruptly and reached for his cane, then remembered with further insult to his dignity that he'd left it upstairs at Willie's insistence. "You don't need that thing when Willie's around," his friend had said, taking care to walk only one step ahead so that Santos could easily follow. Now Willie sensed his friend's discomfort and rose quickly from the table, turning and stepping slowly toward the door. He hoped Santos would come behind him without either one of them having to make a point of it.

When they got back up to the apartment, Willie didn't know what else to do, so he reached out and grabbed Santos' hand and forced it into a shake. "I owe you a lot, you know," he said. "I've gotten a handle on life and what it's all about since I met you, and your lady eagle and her baby."

Santos felt his anger recede. "That is good," he said genuinely, his voice breaking. "Forgive me for my outburst back there. I should be grateful you try to help. I am, Willie, I am grateful. It is just that all my life I knew God intended that I use these hands to capture what my eyes have seen, things of beauty others have missed or feelings they don't know how to express! To fulfill this purpose, I came to America, as I truly believed I was meant to do." He fell back onto the couch and leaned over, his head in his hands. "Now I think I must have dreamed it all up in this hard head of mine! It makes no sense that God would take away the very eyes I need to do what I was meant to do. Suddenly, I am not the man I have known all my life, and I don' know what I'm supposed to do—for myself or for anyone. How do I tell my loved ones that?"

"I know it's tough, Santos. But I guess you just do it. Remember how you kept tellin' me when I was so mad all the time that I was just gonna have to learn how to accept what had already happened and just do what I could to make me better than my old man, not just for everyone else's sake, but especially for mine? That really changed things for me, Santos. It's always harder to do things than just say 'em, but you were really there for me then." Willie turned reluctantly and stepped toward the door. "Now I wanta be there for you. Heck, we might even figure out a way to scrape enough dough together to get you that operation! You'd feel pretty stupid, wouldn't you, seein' clearly again and knowin' you'd wasted all this good time mopin' around?"

Santos couldn't help smiling. "You are a good man, Willie, even if you are a big, fat liar."

"Sometimes," admitted Willie. "But not now. Hey, how would you like a job? I'm gonna go talk to the guys and see what we can figure out. We miss your stubborn temper out there. You sure showed me today you've still got that goin' for you. Heck, maybe we'll turn you into a lackey just to get you back."

"What, a pity job? I don' do pity jobs. You know I have no real purpose in being there any more—or anywhere" he added dolefully.

"After all this, you talk stupid like that? You, of all people, who used to know what life was all about? Ever think maybe your purpose has just changed? Maybe you just have to find out what it is now." Willie opened the door and started out, then turned back, peering around the edge of the door. His bushy red eyebrows furrowed, he opened his mouth and let the thoughts roll out from somewhere deep inside his chest, surprising himself, "Then again, you never know. Maybe your purpose hasn't changed at all. Maybe you're still headin' toward it despite your stubbornness. You just don't know where you're goin' yet. Did you ever think of that?"

Sadder than he let on, but hoping he'd made an impact, Willie closed the door behind him, giving Santos no chance to respond. Santos sat for a long time, listening to Willie's shoes on the stairs, the sidewalk, the street. A truck door closed, a noisy engine turned over. The truck chugged over the cobbled street and into the distance along with the time of day, and life. As they passed, Santos pondered Willie's words, and Marcella's. He hadn't really given up yet, not deep down in his soul. He just couldn't figure out how to make something happen yet. So he didn't do anything all day except strain to watch the shadows of light change, and think a lot, and cry a little, and pray in between.

"You still up there? What you want of me now?" It had been a long time. It wasn't much. But it was a start. He stretched his hands imploringly toward a ceiling he could only trust was there and went on, "What am I suppose to do now? Marcella, Mama', Papa', they all need to know. I need to know. Could you jus' give me, Santos, your servant, some sign so I can pass it on?" He didn't hear an answer. So he got up, felt his way to the bathroom, washed up, felt his way to the bed and plopped down on the lumpy mattress. Seemed like he'd just got up from it. Now here he was again.

34

The boulder had not moved at all. As fate would have it, he remained on the beach where Becky had bid him a loving good-bye. A full moon climbed slowly into the sky and brightened the seemingly ordinary night of continuous motion and change amid the appearance of constancy. Except for the rolling roar of the waves, all was quiet. Everything was in its place, as it was surely meant to be for the moment.

Then, without warning, the sand beside the eagles' boulder billowed up like a tiny volcano. Just as suddenly, the billowing ceased. After a few minutes, it began again, then ceased. The boulder had come to accept surprises. He only wondered what unseen energies were causing such disturbances and what he should brace for now? All through the night the silent commotion, beginning, ceasing, stirring, then stopping, captured the boulder's rapt attention, until the dawn began to stretch its long, graceful arms out against the horizon in a giant yawn. It was almost light when the billowing up in the sand grew stronger, and out poured a sudden current of slow panic, fanning across the beach toward the sea.

Somehow, the boulder knew that this was new life in a frantic rush for survival! Then he realized the rush was created by tiny replicas of the great turtle that had lumbered awkwardly through the sand those many nights ago. Here were hundreds more, in miniature, trying to swim through the sand on webbed legs that were meant for the sea, racing with all their might toward the big world of wetness.

But something had gone terribly wrong! A soundless trumpet must have blown into a thousand terns' ears. With quick, noisy warning, the flapping shadows of feathered wings flocked down on the beach in merciless aim and began to pick off the hatchlings with ravenous hunger.

"No!" cried the boulder. "This is new life! Let it be!"

But the boulder's commands rode on the winds unheeded once more. Soon, less than half of the turtles remained, each dashing in its own path of blind concentration toward the water. "Where is the purpose in this?" cried the boulder. "Did the creature travel the ocean and beach just to feed the terns?"

A few baby turtles that were fast and hearty reached the water's edge. But even as they plunged for cover, the swooping curve of beaks on streaking wings scooped most of them up.

Feeling helpless but desperate to help, the boulder cried out with all his energies, "Please! Let me be more than I am, let me escape these granite bindings. Just this once allow me to see some purpose in their struggle fulfilled!"

A small voice rode in the currents of air flowing past him, "Already at this moment, you are all that you are meant to be. What can be better than that?"

"Whatever I am is not enough!" shouted the boulder. "I need legs, or wings, something else besides myself! Please, for the sake of this new life!"

A sudden prickling worked at his lower sides. Twelve baby turtles blindly seeking survival as all swam in frantic precision deeply into the sand that swirled around the boulder's gaping crevice. Instinctively, they tunneled beneath him, under the same ledge that had served as respite and throne for the dainty child princess.

One tern's round eye caught the movement; he scurried to the boulder and peered under it. Bending low, he angled his head sharply and took aim at the baby turtles with his probing beak.

"Already you are all that you are meant to be, all that you need to be, at this very moment."

The boulder heard. In the stilled moment's reverberating echo, whether or not his substance really grew, his inner existence seemed to swell with caring. Stretch, bend and peck though they tried, several terns failed to penetrate the boulder's protective shield and reach the nervous turtles. Tucked beneath his steadfast presence, the hatchlings hid. Finally, the birds gave up and flew away, searching for easier targets. As soon as night came and draped them with safety, the tiny creatures scrambled out and skittered, unharmed, to the water's edge.

The boulder watched them disappear, one, two, three, four, all twelve, into the destiny that was meant for them.

The next morning, the gold flecks on his granite surface glowed more brightly than ever in the bright sunlight. "Amazing!" he proclaimed. "I only seem like less! In truth, I am more!"

A small voice whispered back, "And not yet all."

35

The boulder's eaglet would never acknowledge that he too might be physically less than he once had been. This unfamiliar helplessness that seemed to threaten his very survival was surely only temporary. Somehow he had made his way onto a rock ledge just above the forest floor, where a few bold streaks of sunlight had pierced their way through the thick screen of pine and danced teasingly over its surface. Now the young tiercel lay weakly but hopefully sprawled on the ledge, wings stretched flat out beside him to absorb as much warmth as possible. Soon, his friend, the sun would drink up this dampness from his feathers, up through its shafts like a boy sipping soda through a straw. Then it could paint its familiar gleam over his wings as he lifted them in easy flight back toward the sky, up and out of this wooded cage to hunt again, to relight all these fading energies.

Then he could find his way once again and fly on toward Eagle Island, as he was meant to do. How grand it would feel to be with others like himself, as his mother had told him, and get rid of these pesky mites that kept stinging the top of his head, where he couldn't reach! Not only were they annoying—they were stealing his power.

But, as if fate answered in cruel denial, the eagle had barely spread his wings out when large gray clouds rumbled in with cold precision, blotting out the tidbits of warmth. The breeze picked up a chill and carried it over the rock ledge. The eagle began to shiver. Closing his eyes, he tried to shut out the chill, to lock in the warmth that still remained in his chest. Sleep stretched its shadows toward him, promising a tempting escape into visions of once-easy pleasures and strength and peace. If only for a moment, he might give in, at least try to re-energize through rest. His eyes closed, ever so slowly. It would be so much easier, just to stay this way...

But the eagle's staunch, enduring spirit would not be stilled. Just as he began to drift off, he somehow knew he must move! Now! Startled into wakefulness, he lifted his wings at an awkward angle, jumped heavily to the ground, and waddled forward, his long, usually adept claws catching on sprawling roots and fallen pine cones, slowing his steps. Straight ahead, though small and distant, a speckle of gray sky winked temptingly, drawing him toward it. Ignoring his weakness and hunger, the grounded eagle heeded his undaunted hope and picked his way over the forest floor. If he could just manage to reach the openness, where the path to the sky was not so impeded—along the way, his feathers would dry, and he could lift himself to the world that was meant to be his before he had lost his way!

Suddenly, a rifle cracked. Wings came to a halt, his body tense. This was a sound he had heard before when humans were near. Death often followed. Quickly, though clumsily, he hopped toward the nearest tree trunk and slid into its shadow. Directly above him, branches snapped in quick succession. Bright snatches of red and bronze bounced against brown-and-gray branches, crashed through all the green pines in its way, and landed with a thud right in front of the surprised eagle. Noisy hounds announced the pheasant's kill and raced across the meadow. Soon they would be upon him!

A lesser bird might, once again and at last, have given up. Instead, he grabbed desperately at his only chance for survival and forced himself into the wind of his own body's resistance, half-flying, half-hopping in endless slow motion toward the still-warm carcass. Pouncing as he once had on a boulder long ago, he tore at a thatch of feathers and laid bare the pheasant's pink skin, dug deftly into the flesh once, twice, one more time just enough to build the energy to hop forward and open his wings in hopeful measure. Not at all to his own amazement, he lifted off and floated silently away just a few feet above the ground.

Bellowing wildly, the unknowing hounds still raced toward the pheasant. Shortly behind them, the hunter followed. Reaching the place where the pheasant had fallen, he stopped short, lifted what remained of the colorful bird, and gazed in shock and disbelief. "What the…?" He turned just in time to see the beginning of the crippled eagle's awkward escape. Carefully, smoothly, he let the pheasant fall beside him and raised the rifle, peering through the sight. Barely stopping, the hounds skidded off at a sharp right angle.

The thought of three noisy dogs tearing after a mighty eagle and bringing it down somehow got to the man. He shouted after them, loud with authority, "Hold your horses, come on back here! No! You leave that poor bird alone!" Lowering the gun, he stared after the fleeing brown streak until its wings opened. Soon the vanishing target was merely a dot, and then gone. He didn't know why he'd let it go, exactly, especially one that had stolen his game; but, those were just the rules, whether formal or not. It had been all he could do not to stand at attention and salute or something. Panting their disappointment, the three dogs padded back to their master and plopped down by his feet. "Well, you guys, they have to eat too!" he said, patting the floppy-eared hound closest to him.

Flying, resting, intermittently hopping and picking his way, the eagle finally reached the open meadow beneath a full sky. His wing was still hampered with pain. His crop was still dangerously empty. But salty moisture tickled his nostrils. Eagle Island must be near! He mustered his last ounce of strength and managed to lift off the ground into the air. Sensing the world of wetness not far away, he headed toward it. Soon he would be where he was meant to be.

36

At that very moment, as Wings struggled to gain altitude, Santos flung his right arm up away from the pillow by his side and down onto the mattress, rolling over and sprawling out flat on his back. It wasn't unusual for the eagle to be riding as it did that morning on the wave of Santos's dreams. Wings and his mother had been on his mind so often since their first dramatic encounter. In sleep, he could still see the eagles clearly, picture them floating across the sky like jets soaring, diving, catapulting straight up with awesome grace and power. He had no conscious awareness of the eaglet's current plight.

Waking with an uneasy start, Santos lay still, staring blankly at the shadows on the ceiling. Something felt especially uncomfortable, but he couldn't put his finger on what it was. He lay there for a long time, trying in earnest to make something of the shadows above him. As a kid, he'd loved to lie on his back in the grass, conjuring out of puffy white clouds monsters and dogs and angels, even God

Himself. How he'd loved that game then! Now, nothing came. Even his imagination was losing its vision.

He didn't remember the dream. As with everything, his memories of the eagles had taken on a melancholy texture. He longed to repeat the dizzying moments he'd shared with them, the constant exhilaration and amazement, a reason for living, the fulfillment of doing something to help even when he hadn't known if he really could. It was different now. He knew he couldn't. How would he climb up to that boulder now, or even be able to find it, or watch the eagles, much less throw fish for them to catch in the air!

People were always trying to help him now. He hated that. He hated that he could hardly even remember what full light had been like, light he had once taken for granted. People who lived in total darkness kept telling him he was still lucky, if only he knew. Be thankful for those shadows, they said. And, someday, he might even see more! Don't get discouraged, how did he think they felt? What if he lost the rest of his sight, wouldn't he wish he had this state back?

He made himself get up before he decided not to, ever again. He made himself go through the motions of eating, washing, getting dressed. He'd promised Willie he'd try to paint. He would go to the beach and try again. With such a vivid dream just now, maybe he could recreate the vision in his mind's eye at least enough to create some wild, abstract representation on canvas not his old way, but something new. Just in case, he tucked an art board and chalks under his arm, picked up his cane, and felt his way out the door. He had counted the steps down to the street long ago, six, seven, all the way to fourteen.

37

The jetty still towered over the eagles' boulder, often casting its long shadow across his surface. His former companions from the mountain seemed to have forgotten him. Many waves carried in by the tides had splashed over him, pounding him ever so slowly deeper into the sand. The boulder had come to accept that this was where he was meant to be, perhaps, until his edges were rounded off by all the forces; eventually, he would be like the tiny rock whose voice he still seemed to hear in the songs of each day. He would never feel the freedom of the gulls or the eagles. Neither baby turtles nor Becky had returned to his place on the sand. But now, he simply allowed himself to be all that he was meant to be, a gift in the gift of each moment.

As such, he drew many others his way. Sometimes they came close and touched him. Others reached out from a distance, as the man with the cane was doing now. All afternoon, he sat on the breakfront, legs dangling over the edge, sending his heavy energy down toward the boulder. This was a man of great significance. The boulder knew that many days ago it was he who had climbed up to hide beneath the boulder and lean upon him to feed the eagles.

But then he had helped to destroy the entire mountain valley, altering their world forever, and carrying the boulder far away from it, along with those the man sat on now! Still, the eagles' boulder had not meant to cause him harm—a thin trace of the man's stain was still etched on his granite. Was he, the boulder, the cause of the man's heavy energies now?

All day, the two sat connected by the wind, exchanging vibrations unaware. Santos had no way of knowing that this was the boulder of so many shared experiences, indeed, a possible cause of his injury. There was nothing apparently significant about the vague, lonely shape on the sand. He just didn't seem to want to try to look any other way, or think about anything else, at the moment. Before he knew it, moments became hours, and then, a whole day. The ball of fire reached the top of its daily ride and started down toward the far edge of the water. The tide called in its larger, more brazen waves to crash threateningly onto the edge of the jetty and over the boulder. With slumped shoulders, Santos pushed himself up, felt for the still-blank canvas and his cane, and slouched back toward his apartment.

He stumbled up the steps two at a time, a small victory he'd claimed last week, two, four, all the way to fourteen.

When he got inside, he plopped right onto the couch, still clutching the canvas against his chest. For a long time, he just sat as he had on the jetty, trying to picture an image to draw. He was so tempted just to give up. Darkness moved up the walls, but it didn't matter. The night was half over before Santos switched on the light and sketched a barren likeness of the mother eagle, a weak charcoal outline, no genuine attempt at capturing her majesty. He couldn't give up yet. Maybe tomorrow he'd throw in some colors, haphazardly let them fall where they may. Who could tell what he might create, and who would be drawn to it? Crazier things had happened.

The next day, Santos returned to the breakfront above the eagles' boulder, as he was meant to do, and propped himself and the art board at its uppermost level, leaning into a deep crevice. Passionate strains of Ravel marched through his mind as he grabbed for colors at random, smearing them recklessly across the canvas, trying to capture the motion of the eagles' wings with broad strokes, red, and then yellow, and green, and magenta—all without being certain what colors he used. Perhaps this was how Picasso and Pollack had created some of their masterpieces. Perhaps he even touched slightly on Van Gogh's madness, as he attempted in vain to let the paint speak of his mounting anger, the frustration of this sudden, unnatural limitation that seemed so unfair, such an insult to his talent and his purpose, as if he were just a toy for God to play with and to tease.

Hours later, even though he wasn't sure what he'd really accomplished, Santos decided he'd done enough to learn whether he still had something to offer. Rolling the chalk back into its pack, he set his creation up next to him on display and leaned back, waiting. People were always passing by as they hiked out to the rock peninsula's farthest point. Santos knew from past experience if they liked his work, they would stop, possibly even comment, if not to him, to their companions.

He waited for the rest of the afternoon. A few people paused beside him. He heard some whispers, but the only words he could decipher were "look" and "that man" and "mmm hmmm." Probably, they were whispering of their pity. He finally got fed up with them and himself. He jumped up so fast he almost lost his balance, as he grabbed a corner of the canvas and flung it as far as he could out into the water. Hearing it splash, he stood for awhile, his face open to the mist, picturing his work and his heart just bobbing there, riding the waves into shore like a Styrofoam board. Then, soaked and reshaped beyond recognition, it would be carried back out into the huge black void in the ocean's vast middle.

With as much dignity as he could muster, he turned and aimed himself toward the small apartment that was fast becoming his hiding place. Who was he, anyway, to think he was meant for something special? He was only an ordinary man after all, one of many. He was sure now if he were meant to do more with his art, his sight would not have been taken away. He planted his feet with firm determination, struggling for the acceptance he knew he must reach if he was to survive at all. He was only an ordinary man. He must accept these limitations, set new goals, be open to a new purpose no matter how humble, or how far from his creative heart.

At least, he could take the steps up to his flat two at a time now without using his cane. He'd already memorized their shape and size. Maybe Willie would come back tomorrow and offer him that job he'd talked about. Whatever it was, he would say yes and be glad. Santos would do what he could for his loved ones. Tonight, he would manage to scrawl a letter to Marcella and tell the truth. He would tell her it might not be much, but he would do what he could do if she still wanted to come to America, and she and Mama' and Papa' could still get away. He would do what little he could to help them here, even if Marcella no longer wanted him.

38

The boulder had sensed the man's anguish. Again, he was reminded of the mark of shame upon his surface caused by the man's pain and his own repulsion. He longed to reach out, to erase the damage he'd done, and he tried, really tried, just as he'd tried to lighten his weight and be carried to the fire rings. Nothing happened. The man was altered forever, just like the mountain and the boulder itself.

Of course, the man had played his part too—he wasn't completely free of guilt. Why should the boulder have to bear it all? Everything had changed because of this man and the other humans. If anything, he should try to help the boulder!

Likely chance. Doubtful they would ever be able to help one another ever again or make things right again. The boulder's new awareness changed nothing, really. Here he was, after all, just a big hunk of granite, trapped in the sand, unable to move or emote or help or be helped. "I might as well just sit here, stop fooling myself, and let the forces do what they will with me," he concluded. "They're going to, anyway. What power do I have to alter things now?"

He began to reclose the pores on his surface, one by one, once and for all. He had allowed himself to become far too vulnerable. "The forces don't care about me," he declared. "Why should I care about me? And why should I care what happens to others? Noble purpose, indeed. I am a rock, a lopsided slab of granite slowly being shaped by forces out of my control. I might as well give up and let it happen. I am going to sleep again."

But awareness once wakened never sleeps long. The surprise of existence, once fully appreciated, lights the way for the recognition of surprises always forthcoming. A small voice drifted in through the boulder's surface. "At this very moment, the most of what you have to give continues into the universe, even as did your least. The world within you is no longer small nor empty. Each moment, therefore, is your most. Stars are the boulders of the sky. You are a star of the sand! Allow yourself to shine! You are not yet all!" The voice drifted away in a gale of laughter shaped in a swirl of tiny giggles. There was no doubt in the boulder's awareness whose voice it had been. There was only doubt in the meaning of its words.

"Show me what you mean! How am I to be all?"

Darkness fell. A bright full moon slightly warmed the crisp night, but no more humans ventured onto the beach, having escaped its chill into the warm security of their homes. Suddenly, a draft moved in and hovered directly above the boulder. A cold form sank its full weight onto his granite, sending a shudder throughout his existence. Limply draping huge wet wings down the boulder's sides, the creature lowered its head to rest, body trembling. As its life energies seeped through the boulder's outer layers and forced through his pores into the depths of his existence, the boulder realized with shocked awareness that this was the youngest bearer of wings ever to rest a deadly talon upon his surface, the eagle he had once shared the hard, hot womb of the mountain mother with.

He forgot not to care. "What has happened to you, old friend?" he cried out.

There was no response. The eagle's rhythm of life beat faintly against him. "I feel your weakness, but I know your strength! Please, mighty bird, do not give up!"

Against his will, the boulder found himself yearning to lighten as well as lift, to embrace as well as support. But, still, he was trapped by his limitations, thoughts traveling only patterns of his own understanding. Here he was again, the world around him blotted out by a limp body, its faint heart beating against his surface. But this time, he had no concern for the effect on his own existence. "Hang on!" he cried, trying to reach beyond his own realm into the eagle's. "Your purpose still lies before you, I am sure of it! You cannot give up! It is I, the boulder refuge you once sought! You learned to survive upon my back once before! Survive again!"

Whether or not he heard, the determined bird lifted his gaze and stretched his neck longingly eastward. For a brief moment, his head swayed back and forth like a wary snake surmising the threat of its environment. Then it dropped again, resting flat out on his old friend. *How had he gotten here? Was he back on the mountain? Was this the same rock throne he had claimed as home so long ago? How very long ago that was! How far away! Why had he seemed to be drawn here by an unseen force? He'd only rested a moment on that big rock ledge over there and then tried once again to project his bullet-like torso across the water. He was sure his destination was near. But when he'd tried to push off from the ledge, the air had not lifted him, as it had before! He simply could go no further.*

"Hear me, winged one!" called the boulder, sensing the eagle's defeat. He tried to shine like a star on the sand, to emit the same caring that had seemed to swell his being for the new turtles; he had grown enough to provide refuge for them to help them survive! Surely, he could do the same for the eagle! The sea encroached more and more. The eagle now lay completely inert, not even trying to escape. The boulder longed to move back from the water with the bird on his back. He begged once more for his own wings so he could lift them both to the skies.

The boulder didn't know how to rekindle the eagle's energies, to reignite the indomitable spirit that had been his.

He didn't know how to save him or help him save himself. But, oh, how he wanted to! Nevertheless. A powerful claw of a wave reached up and swiped the eagle off the boulder into the black wetness. There was no cry, no objection, no threat of retaliation by the eagle.

Only the boulder matched the sea's broiling intensity. *"Why could I not have been more? The eagles were a part of the mountain, part of me, the boulder that laced the mountain's side, throne to many families of eagles! Why could I not save him? Does he just cease to exist now? Is his significance limited to the sand on which he lies now? Is this what you meant, small rock?"*

Only the waves roared an answer. Once again, the boulder battled with acceptance and parried with truth, though he knew too well its unyielding constancy. Why could he not be enough? Why could he not have shot skyward with the eagle on his back, a geyser of granite refuge and escape? Had he truly been all that he could be? Was the eagle's purpose truly complete, or had it been snuffed out by the forces just for their pleasure, their whim? Were they laughing at him? Crying? Feeling anything at all, taking away an existence so magnificent?

And when would the glow of acceptance such as he had known and felt so recently be eternally shielded from all the ill-winds of the universe? When would he stop reeling against the constancy of change and loss?

39

Santos was struggling as well, trying to put proper words onto paper. He could hardly see the words he could barely bring himself to write.

Dear Marcella, Mama and Papa,

I regret it is so long. Some things are the same, like my heart. But Santos cannot see or earn money with his heart. And some things are different, like my eyes and what they see..."

What would he say next, "I guess I drank too much tequila one night, and I went for a walk on some slippery rocks by the ocean to escape this red-haired siren, and...well, I traded one danger for another...but please believe me, I was thinking of you, Marcella, and how we would all be together again soon, just before I fell..."

It sounded so very bad. He couldn't find the words in his head or see them on the paper well enough to know if what he did get down was readable. Five times he started, then five times more, but each paper was crumpled and thrown aside on the floor, the table, the couch where he sat.

Maybe the night air would clear his head. Maybe he'd even feel more normal in the dark. He grabbed his jacket and cane and went down the stairs as fast as he could. Such small pleasures now. What grand prize did he think he was, anyway, to ask them to face the sea's dangers without him, then somehow manage to make it here with the little support he could now give? Would they think he just needed someone to take care of him? Never! He would rather die first.

"How can you talk that way, Santos, say such things in God's earshot?" His Mother's voice played in the wind, as clearly scolding him now as it had whenever he'd said a foul word as a kid. He walked forward, just following his cane and the sounds of the ocean. When its salty mist stung his nose, he stood tall and straight, letting it seep through all his senses. He'd never noticed how the water hissed when it hit the sand. Every sound was a little bit different, the song and the movement constant, yet changing with every wave. Like life. If only he could get used to it. Did anyone? Some people seemed to have it so easy, like people born in America. Just lucky. He'd been fooling himself all along. Life just happened, just a roll of the dice, and you play out what you get the best you can. Or you throw away your future by doing something stupid, like trying to navigate the jetty

at night with a tequila brain! How could he have been so careless with God's gifts? Maybe this was just punishment, after all. But he was not the only one being punished.

He didn't feel like hiking the jetty. A walk on the beach, maybe, if the tide hadn't gobbled up too much of the sand. He sat on his haunches and slid down the sandy bank. The water swished around his ankles immediately. The thought occurred to him, *Still being stupid in the dark.* But it didn't really matter now. He sloshed through the water, struggling to maintain his balance against its swirling forces. The incoming waves roared at his ears like angry lions, matching his mood. He lifted his face to the heavy mist and let it wash over him.

The boulder seemed to rise up out of nowhere. Santos bumped into it, banging his chin on its only point, where the granite had been chipped off the night of the storm.

"Ow! Watch where you're going!" Santos blurted, irritated, and not quite sure whether he was talking to himself or the boulder. "Stupid," he added out loud, half to reassure himself of his sanity. Reaching out, he touched the rock in curiosity, rubbing his hand across it. This must be the same rock he'd been staring at all day yesterday, just down from the jetty. He couldn't see it any better now than he could then. It was just a dark blob. Why did it seem so familiar?

Well, that was silly. It was probably part of the mountain he'd carted here himself. Maybe it was reaching out to get back at him. Maybe everything that was happening to him was just reward for all the damage he'd helped to do to that whole place, the mountain, the eagles, the boulders, everything. They'd all been there so many years before he and his gang had come along. Yeah, they were just trying to earn a living, even build a road to freedom for themselves and their loved ones. But who did they think they were, casually obliterating what had been standing for so long through so many ages, placed there by God's mighty hand?

Reason told him that a rock was a rock, and that was that. But as his fingers, more sensitive now, rubbed back and forth, Santos knew they had met before, *Could this be the eagles' boulder, the one he'd climbed on to bring them food?* There had been no jagged edge to it then. But he knew only too well change can happen in an instant. And though he had dumped all the rocks on top of the jetty himself, he knew a crane had followed and moved them all around for even coverage. But boulders didn't just tumble down from a breakfront, even in hurricane winds. How had this guy wound up on the sand all by himself like this?

For some crazy reason deep within, Santos recognized that this was the eagles' boulder. "You are much older than I, friend boulder!" Santos said aloud. "Probably you could share many stories of years gone by. Would you come right out and tell me if you hated me? Or would you just reach out and strike me blind? Or," he added with a chuckle, "would you drive me insane and make me talk to you so you wouldn't have to stan' here all lonely like me?"

Leaning back into the boulder's crevice, the same one Becky had sought refuge in, Santos slid impulsively down its slick wet surface and lay back against it in the sand. As waves crashed loudly all around him, Santos kept talking, letting words roll out as he never would have dared in the company of another human being or even to a boulder without the sea's voice dwarfing his own. "I am so sorry I take you away from your home country, that I steal your freedom to fin' my own. Now we both have lost the freedom. What do you think about that? Do you think I should just give up and end it, here and now? Would that make you feel better? You are still a thing of great substance, a thing of significance even away from your mountain. But, me, Santos, what good am I, a blind artist far from my homeland? One who was vain enough to believe he was special, that God Himself had gifted him with lofty purpose? An' then to throw it all away with one night of stupidity! Now I must give up on all those big dreams I smashed, don' you think?"

No! You cannot give up!" the boulder wanted to answer. To the forces that had made him, he cried out once more on behalf of another, "Not him too, please! Do not take this man! Surely, he still has much to give. Is my existence now only to lead to others' destruction? Is that to be my true significance?"

Neither he nor Santos heard an answer to their pleas, other than the ocean's never-ending roar. Maybe that was their answer. If Santos sat here long enough, the water would just keep working its way up to the boulder, then around it, like it was doing now deeper and deeper, soaking his shoes and pants. Shivering, he felt his cane bump up against him, but he had no energy or desire to retrieve it. Too bad—if his cane washed out to sea, like that thing he had tried to call art had probably done today, he would have nothing to lean on at all. No way to find his way in life at all.

And if the water came up far enough that it washed him out, too, while he was just sitting here minding his own blind business, well, then, could God really blame him? Maybe God wanted him in heaven now, anyway, to paint the angels. He could probably see and paint again there. Maybe that was his purpose all along. He was just on his natural way to paint the angels for God. Then again, would God let him in? Did he deserve it?

Another wave made it up around the boulder and crept over Santos' legs. He pushed back against the granite, bracing himself. Maybe he'd get up after this one. He hadn't decided yet. Maybe he'd just decide not to decide at all, and just let things happen. Arms dangling, palms up on the sand, Santos waited for a sign, some good reason to save himself.

In a hoarse whisper, he cast his blind eyes toward the sky and moaned aloud, "I guess it is time that I give up the fight. That is what you want, yes? You want me up there to paint your angels, like Michelangelo did down here?" Then he added quickly, "Forgive me. I know I am no Michelangelo. I am ashamed to have claimed such a thing!"

The boulder sensed the man's desperation, felt the same heaviness as when the man had slipped on him so long ago before the storm. The man's energies seemed to be slipping from him again as they had that night—and yet, these were a different kind of energy, not tangible. Nevertheless. Must he always sit passively by while those who came to him for support found only hard granite to lean on as they came to an end before their time?

"No!" he cried out to the forces once more. "Let the man continue! Let me be more than I seem to be, more than I am, all that I can possibly be. Let me help this life continue, as it is surely meant to do!"

As if in answer to them both, a slimy heap suddenly rode a wave in and slapped against them, cold and hard, scaring Santos half out of his wits. A soggy heaviness wrapped around him like seaweed preparing a gift to carry back out to the sea. Was this death itself, coming to wrap its clammy fingers around him and carry him to his end? Santos tried to stay limp, but his whole body went rigid. Jarred into alertness, he leaped up. "What the…?" Was it a jelly fish? Had he already been stung? More like a squid.

Weren't they poisonous if they got you just right? So what did he care? Wasn't he just giving up a minute ago?

Or was everything just a bad dream, and he was still on the island, and he could still see? He leaned down toward where he'd been sitting, squinting. No, he couldn't see much, only a blob. He reached out with a timid finger and touched it. Were those wet feathers?

"It's a dead bird!" he exclaimed. "I think!" Cautiously, he reached out, placed his palm over the blob's middle. Did it still have a heartbeat, or were the waves just moving it around? "Are you really a gonner? Or are you jus' hurt? Do you need the help maybe?" He had to chuckle to himself, remembering how Jake had called him Mr. Tender Mercy.

"Yeah, well, that is okay. I am what I am," he whispered, thankful to set his own troubles aside and feeling suddenly silly for overreacting to what some might think were small problems. Maybe this was God's answer, like a good papa slap, admonishing, "Wake up! Don't be glum! Be happy! Help, not hurt!"

Anyway, something didn't want Santos giving up yet. He reached deeply into the sand beneath the heap of feathers and tried to lift up.

"Carumba! The water makes you heavy!" He could have left it there. This would be a decent burial ground for a bird of the sea. But, somehow, Santos seemed reborn himself, his old curiosity keeping him going like it always did. This was a big bird, not a seagull. Maybe a pelican. It was almost too heavy to lift.

"You can do it!" the boulder tried to convey, having been keenly aware of everything that had happened.

Santos didn't appear to hear. Another wave washed up, knocking him off his feet. It picked up the heap of feathers and carried it back out into the darkness.

"Wait!" cried Santos.

"No!" the boulder cried out.

The wave swooped back toward them. Before Santos knew what hit him, the soggy mass of heavy feathers had been dropped right down into the cradle of his outstretched arms, as if he were an open front loader.

"Whoa! Now what am I...." Never mind. This was meant to be; it couldn't be denied now. Santos stood up as straight as he could under its weight, fighting the urge to drop it, at least to push its heavy clamminess away from his own prickly skin. Shaking from the cold now, he stumbled his way up to dry sand and laid his burden gently on the rocks above. Putting his face up close to its head, he squinted in the moonlight, trying to see what it was.

The eagle opened its eyes and stared wildly into his. It struggled weakly under his touch. Santos couldn't believe what he thought he was seeing. Was his imagination getting the best of him? Was he just waking up, still on the island, and everything in between had been only a nightmare?

This sure seemed like a real eagle, and its heart was beating faintly right under the palm of his own real hand. But was anything real anymore?

Just in case, he pushed down on the bird's chest gently, wondering if you could save a drowning bird the same way as humans.

Then he scooped it up and held it close to him like a baby, buckling under its soggy weight and quickly discarding the worry of any possible threat still posed by its beak or disease. Not sure how he'd get there, Santos turned away from the ocean toward his apartment. He wouldn't be able to use his cane, even if he could find it. But there was nowhere else to go now in the middle of the night, and they both had to get in out of the cold. All the way, he was wondering, *Was all this even possible, an eagle in his arms, an eagle washed up by the ocean? No one would believe it! Not even Willie!*

There was the boardwalk, wood under his feet, good. He began shuffling his feet, like all the blind people he'd pitied before, just ahead of his steps, testing for cracks and curbs, one, two, one more to go, and then the corner, the bottom door, fourteen steps, and his door at the top. He reached in his pocket holding his breath, hoping the key hadn't washed out with the swirling waters, managing to cradle the eagle's head against his neck as he leaned back to hold it up with his other arm. He'd gone crazy, for sure. For all he really knew, he was bringing a sick vulture into his house, and he'd be attacked in the middle of the night, when he was fast asleep! Or he'd die of some horrible bird disease.

Too tired to worry now, he slammed the door shut with his foot, still holding tight to the bird, whatever it was, until he leaned over and laid it right on the floor just as it was. He stumbled to the closet, pulled out a towel, and wrapped it around the still eagle, hoping it would be enough to warm and dry it, as well as shield it from the cold, hard floor. Completely spent, his mind whirling like a cement mixer, he collapsed his own body flat out on the bed and pulled the blanket up over his head. Just in case. Tomorrow—if he was still alive, and the bird was too— they would both feel better. Then, if it still didn't strike out and kill him first, he could think better about what to do.

40

The next thing he knew, Willie was banging on the door, demanding in his loud tenor voice, "Hey! Santos! You in there, can you hear me? It's Willie, come on, it's time to go to work! Your lazy days are over! Let me in!"

Santos woke up with a start. What a dream that had been! He jumped up faster than he had for a long time, though his muscles ached as if he'd been hit by a truck. Had it been a dream? He checked the floor. There was the towel, a lumpy stretch on the floor. He bent over, made himself grab the edge, and peeked underneath. The young eagle's eyes flung open wide and stared into Santos' face. Santos went rigid as he stared back, wondering again if he really was deciphering the shape of an eagle's head. And if he shouted an answer to Willie, who was still pounding impatiently on the door, would he be taking a chance of losing a nose or one of these useless eyes? What had he been thinking last night? Had he had too much tequila again? Had he really brought a dying bird up to his room? Or had he finally succumbed to that redhead, and she'd been transformed by the *brujeria*! He was loco, yes. They were all right to call him that after all.

Willie jiggled the doorknob. To his surprise, it turned in his hand. He stormed in.

"Shhhh" warned Santos, leaning over the towel.

"What's that?" Willie rushed over, grabbed the corner of the towel, and flung it back, as if he wanted to rescue Santos from whatever was underneath it. The eagle stirred only slightly, but its eyes were bright and bulging, wide open. Startled, Willie threw the towel back over it. Jerking away, he rubbed at his own eyes, taking giant strides back toward the door.

"What the heck? What'd you do, Santos, have some more tequila last night and go swimmin' with the…" He had to tiptoe back to confirm what he'd seen, this time gently lifting only a corner of the towel to peek beneath it. "Am I seein' things? Or did you go and find Mama Eagle again?"

"I don' know, is it Mama, is it Wings, or am I just the eagle magnet? You see better than I do. Can you tell, is the head white, like the Mama's? But whoever, whatever, this eagle is sick. Can you fin' it a doctor?"

"Man, if that don't take the cake. How'd it get up here? Fly through the window? How'd it find you?"

"We sort of find each other," said Santos, sinking down on the bed, shaking his own head in disbelief. "You wanna hear somethin' really weird? We fin' each other by the boulder! I mean, I think maybe it was the same boulder that was their home on the mountain!"

"What, you went back there and found—?" Willie stopped himself. "How could either one of you tell one rock from another down by the jetty?"

"I don' know, Willie, I can't explain anythin'. All I know is, we are both there at the same time, an' so was this big rock, an' it seems like we both get pulled to it, sort of like bein' pulled to home! Do you know somebody in town, maybe, a doctor of the animals? It is here now, we got to do somethin'!"

"I'll see what I can do!" Willie hollered, spinning around and darting back through the door. He'd never raced down any stairs so fast. Running right past the truck, he bolted straight toward the office of the only doctor he knew in town, the one who'd helped Santos the night he'd slipped on the rocks. He didn't know of any vets around; anyway, if they had both gone off the deep end, at least this doctor would know what had started it. How in the world could that have been one of their eagles? They should be far away by now, happy and strong and flying free in their new home, way inland from here. His heart sank. At least, that was what they'd all figured.

Santos only knew he wasn't going to disturb whatever this was, and he sure was glad Willie kept turning up, even when he should mind own business. He waited, fighting the urge to move around for what seemed like hours, rubbing his hand reassuringly over the eagle's feathers. They were drier now, but he could still feel the dampness. He knew it was really sick, or it would be going wild by now. Or did it know he wouldn't hurt it, because it knew him, because this really was Mama Eagle or maybe even Wings?

"Ah, if it is really you, then we come full circle, you and I, no?" he whispered. "Our paths seem destined to cross again and again!"

And so it was that the very man who had been wondering about the value of his own life the night before now found himself hoping and praying for the life of an eagle. "Don' die, beautiful eagle!" he begged. "I would never be able to forgive myself if I caused you such harm!"

Finally, Willie came back, and they wrapped the near-lifeless form in the towel. Dr. Mueller had said he didn't know much about sick eagles, and they'd probably all be better off if Santos had just left it where it was. But he'd agreed to do what he could for now, and if it lived long enough, he'd try to bring in someone who knew a lot more about eagles than he did.

When the moment came, Santos whispered reassurance. "You will be all right, my friend! The doctor is very good. He took good care of Santos, he will take good care of you too, fix your wing, give you food, water, medicine, whatever you need. Soon you will be restored to your rightful place in the sky." The eagle, sprawled with wings out flat on the cage floor, gave no sign of caring, one way or the other. Santos turned and made his way out to the truck, where Willie was waiting, leaning against it.

They were both swiping at their eyes as they opened their doors and stepped up into the truck. For a good ten minutes, they just sat there, only their minds racing ahead. "You know, no matter how this thing turns out, you and me and the eagles, we're all intertwined somehow," Willie announced as he turned the key and steered away from Sand Harbor. "You sure have shown me what it's all about. It's like you took this aggravating, meaningless thing I used to think life was and plastered it across this big canvas of yours, bein' an artist, and all in these bright new colors I'd never seen before, you know what I mean?" Not waiting for an answer, he rambled on with the roll of the tires toward the mountain, where it had all begun, "Then you aimed the floodlights right at it, full force, you know? I mean, I'd never thought a thing about this purpose you keep talkin' about, and I'm still wonderin' what mine is, if I even have one, other than just to live it a day at a time. But you've already fulfilled yours as far as I'm concerned."

"Oh! Thanks, Willie, I guess my time is up, then?" Santos joked, taking a grateful whiff of the mountain air. He loved the ocean air too, wet with the heavy stench of fish and salt, but this sage and lavender traveled lightly, barely teasing his nostrils. "So you think you have nothin' to do with the survival of Santos and of Mama Eagle and her baby? Or we don' show up on this big canvas of yours? Do you know how close we just come to being painted out?" He leaned his head at a sharp angle, completely out the open window, aiming his nose toward the sky, dunking his face fully into the wind, almost giddy from its pungent perfume.

"So what work do I do when we get there? You got real work or pity work?"

"Yeah, yeah, yeah. You'd have found a way, Santos, you know you would have. I only came in after the fact to do what I could. And don't worry, you'll earn your keep. But did you know I don't feel like white-knucklin' everything I see any more, thanks to you and those birds of yours? I feel like I'm still me, in the same skin, but everything inside is different. You know how some horses have to wear blinders to keep from getting' spooked by everything around 'em?"

Santos nodded, trying not to acknowledge his growing discomfort from Willie's analogies.

"Well that was me. Only my blinders made me crazier, not calmer. I mean, I couldn't see the whole puzzle of this amazing world and all the little things that make it up 'cause I was so mad all the time all I wanted to do was kick at any of those things that blew past me or got in my line of vision. You know what I mean?" Not getting an answer, he shot a quick glance toward his friend.

Santos sat rigid now, face straight ahead, jaw set tightly on his square chin. "Oh, Lord, Santos," Willie moaned.

"Leave it to me to find somethin' stupid to say! How could I go on like that and not even hear myself?"

"Do you think I wan' my friends to be afraid to say things right out, afraid it might make me cry like the baby? No, Willie! An' anyway, I know you speak in metaphors. An' anyway, only my physical vision is injured. I still 'see' very well with the heart an' the brain."

"Okay," said Willie, relieved for the moment. "Then what do you think about what I was sayin'?"

"I think that only a wise man of courage learns to offer the open palm once he is used to the fist. Why is it people who can see so much better than I can with their eyes seem to see so much less than I do? Only reacting, never stopping to think? It is a turn of the soul, am I right? It is what you managed to do, that your poor papa did not."

"Ahhh, my old man ain't poor, he's just hard-headed. I'm not even sure he's even got a heart! He would never..." Willie stopped midsentence, deep in thought as he aimed the truck over the gravel road they had laid themselves— he and Santos and the others. It seemed such a short time ago. How could so much have happened? He turned the wheel into the curve that would lead them straight to the mountain, kicking up dust. When they made it through to the other side, maybe he'd go see how the old guy was doing, just for the heck of it.

41

Even Hank seemed glad to have Santos back. He hustled right over to the truck, huddling in like one of the guys, waiting his turn to shake his hand. He didn't go all out and hug him, like a few of the men did, with honest affection. Santos grinned broadly, trying not to act self-conscious.

"So what work do I do?" he blurted out, hoping to break his own tension. "You got pity work or real work?"

The whole group came to awkward attention. There were a few guffaws, the clearing of throats, louder than seemed natural.

"Well, you may not be able to do all the things you used to do, Santos," Jake admitted right out, placing a hand on his shoulder and nudging him toward camp. "But we'll see you have an honest day's labor, don't worry. Have you ever seen me let anyone get by with anything less?"

"What, you mean I have to wash dishes?"

Embarrassed laughter worked its way through the huddle of men shuffling behind Jake and Santos. "Say, I don't remember, are you any good at dishes?" challenged Jake, coming right to the point he knew Santos was asking for.

"You show me the job. I will do it better than anyone here—especially Willie!" Santos chided, hiding behind an even wider grin. Again, he was gratified by doting laughter.

"Nah, we've got worse things than washin' dishes. Come on, I'll show you."

The rest of the week, Santos shoveled and raked gravel, carried firewood, even managed to hook a few willing trout on the end of his fly rod, learning to lean more and more into sounds and smells and weights and surfaces. When he did wash dishes, he made sure the bubbles were thick, the water silky, the plates smooth to the feel. He noticed that nobody corrected his efforts out loud, but sometimes he could hear them behind him, reworking his results. It wasn't that the work was so insulting, though the tightness in his chest revealed even to his stubborn pride how much he hated his stilted abilities and made him wonder if he'd ever really get used to them.

Worst of all, he just couldn't stop thinking about the eagle. "It is still alive, I am sure," he announced, reassuring himself when they'd finally made it through the week, and he and Willie were headed back to Sand Harbor early Friday afternoon.

"You bet," his friend responded confidently.

But as Dr. Mueller ushered them back to the makeshift cage in the storage room, Willie couldn't help but wail, "Oh, man!"

There on a perch behind the bars was a thin, ragged replica of the grand eagle they had known. It hardly moved as the three men approached, keeping its beak tucked in at the tip of its right wing, the once-regal head hidden, except for the very top, where prickly pink skin, barren of feathers, was exposed. The eagle's left wing hung by its side, braced by a neat row of wooden tongue depressors.

"I think I'm glad you can't see her too good," Willie admitted. "Will she make it, Doctor?"

"It's still hard to tell, gentlemen, though I think you should know this is no lady."

"Really? It is a male? Can you tell how old?"

"Well, not exactly, but he's a young one, no doubt less than a year. Guess that's how he got in trouble—lack of experience against the elements."

"Then it is Wings, the baby eagle on the rock! Doctor, we are this eagle's uncles! We throw him the fish, teach him to fly, to eat, to survive in the wild when we had to roust him and his Mama out from the mountain home!"

Santos' face fell. "Guess we are not the good teachers we think we are. All we do for him is harm, make him think he will be okay and…"

224

"You tried, gentlemen. That's all you could do. Like myself. You know, I can only do so much too. But the Singleton Zoo returned my call. He probably won't ever be what he might have been, and it's doubtful he'll ever fly again. But they think they might be able to help him regain—"

"A zoo?" cried Willie.

"Such a magnificent bird caged forever?" challenged Santos.

"I'm sorry," the doctor replied gently. "But he's really been dehydrated and underfed for too long, and he seems to have lost his appetite. That's not good for a big bird like this. I just don't have the time or the resources."

"How much in American dollars? I am working again now, perhaps I can offer—"

"I'm afraid it would be more than you…"

"Okay. I take care of him myself. If he has to die in his heart, let him really die, with dignity, in the freedom that has always been his. That is what he is all about. I will take care of him. I buy from you what he needs, okay? You tell me…"

Dr. Mueller didn't allow him to finish. Clasping his hands behind his back, he turned away and walked back toward his office, head down. Santos mourned at the sound of his retreat. Completely discouraged, not knowing what to do, he and Willie just stood there leaning on the bars, holding silent vigil. Willie was trying to get up the nerve to suggest they give up for now and take off, when the doctor returned.

"You know, Santos, I've been needing an extra pair of hands for longer than I care to admit. I couldn't pay much more than bare wages, but if you'd like to help me out with odd jobs around here, maybe we could bring that eagle around to better health together. He obviously means a lot to you, and he trusts you. Would you be interested?"

"Yahoo!" Santos yelled. "Would I! Once again, I live for a reason!" Grabbing out for both Willie and the doctor, he wrapped each of them in a big bear hug, declaring, "You bet I can do it! We can do it! Teamwork!" In afterthought, he added, "Willie, you think it is okay with Hank and the others?"

"If it's not, I'll set 'em straight! We all wanna see 'Wings' fly again, even Hank. And Santos—it sure is good to hear that dumb 'yahoo!' of yours again."

"Yeah? Well, then, let's teach Wings his name." He reached out, latched on to the bars of the cage, and leaned in, directing his voice toward the shadow before him, "Wings, you hear? Might as well get used to it—and, get ready to use what you are named for, no? You got to live up to your name, no?"

"Yeah! Not no! Yeah!"

Dr. Mueller interrupted, cautioning, "Whoa there, let's not put the horse before the cart. Only time will tell." Seeing their faces fall, he added, "But you obviously like a good challenge, and so do I. We'll all do our best."

42

Santos didn't mind scrubbing the cage, mopping all the floors, folding laundry over and over, nearly as much as he'd minded doing the mundane chores at camp. He memorized every inch of the halls, where furniture and lab pieces were, doors, windows, every bar on the makeshift cage. Every day, he offered his winged friend tempting leftovers from the butcher down the street, dicing the meat into chunks with only a few choice bits of his fingers going into the dish. Every day, he'd open the cage door and shuffle cautiously toward its sound and smell, holding the dish at arm's length in front of him. The big gloves Dr. Mueller had given him for protection sat on the counter, ignored. Someday, he kept telling himself, he could do this without his skin getting prickly, wondering when the eagle would push off from his perch and fly at his face, and he wouldn't even know until it had sliced into his skin, revived and angry at the person it might deem its captor.

Wings continued to ignore the food and Santos, his beak tucked tightly into his thinning feathers. "What, this food's not good enough for you? Not like your Mama's cookin'?" The eagle's shadow remained motionless. Suddenly, a new thought dawned on Santos. "Dummy!" he grumbled, slapping his forehead with his open palm. "Why I don' think of this before?" He made a beeline to the butcher shop on the edge of town in the middle of the day. "You got any fresh trout?" he asked, leaning on the counter for support.

"Yeah, but it'll cost you a buck."

Santos dug in his pocket, sifted out four quarters, and plopped them on the counter. One way or another, he was going to save that eagle, even if he had to force-feed him. Setting up a portable table in front of his perch, he opened the paper and placed it on the table, exposing the trout. He dug right in through the thick layer of skin with his fingers, worked through the bones and mush, picked out a healthy chunk, and held it right up, touching the eagle's beak with the side of his hand. He was pretty sure it could still break his fingers or chop them off and chew them, if it wanted to. He held his breath, bracing for the worst. To his astonishment, the eagle reached right in, plucked the fish meat out of his grasp without a scratch to his bare skin and seemed to swallow it down.

"That's the way, Wings," Santos whispered, gulping down his own excitement. "Here, wan' some more?"

He'd barely reached up when his fingers were empty. Bite after bite, they worked together, building a rhythm. "Wow. How 'bout that! You do remember, don' you, Wings? You live up to your name again soon, right? You like this good ol' trout, fresh from the stream? Tomorrow, I will bring you more. And every day, as long as it takes, until I can leave it for you, the whole fish, like a banquet before you to feast on all by yourself. Ah yes, and I will even throw it high in the air for you, and you can soar up to catch it midair! Then, someday, you will grow strong again and catch your own fish! Then you don' need Santos no more."

Already, he was beginning to have mixed feelings. The day came when the eagle lifted his wings and slowly eased them down, then lifted them, again, and again. As he began to exercise them more in earnest, he whipped up a wind in Santos's stomach, as well as all around the cage. Pretty soon, he'd be able to fly free, just what Santos wanted. Didn't he? Why was he so sad? The big bird didn't scare him a bit any more, even when he flapped at Santos wildly. Inevitably, the day they'd been working toward unveiled its gift of a brilliant morning before them. Santos could no longer stall. Steeling himself with a deep breath, he wrapped a tether around the eagle's leg. On this big occasion, he felt for the glove on the counter, picked it up, and thrust his hand into it before opening the cage door and reaching in toward the eagle. With a soft, throaty sound, Wings climbed willingly on to his gloved hand, just as they'd practiced. But this time, Santos left the cage door open, turned, and shuffled slowly forward, his arm muscles tensed and strained under the weight of the eagle. Dr. Mueller marched behind them, ready to spring into action, if necessary. They'd barely made it through the door when Wings stretched out eagerly, as he was meant to do, and lifted off toward the familiar open sky. Only the wire stopped his climb. Though it surprised him, he circled around and allowed himself to be coaxed back in.

"This time, anyway," Santos told Willie on the phone that night. "He is ready to take off for good. I am not ready. But I believeWings is."

They decided to take him back to the mountain. The valley was home to him. "Maybe he just wasn't able to nestle into anything new for keeps, jus' like me," Santos suggested.

"He could probably nest nearby, now that the blasting is done," offered Willie. "He might be lonely for awhile, and it wouldn't be what he was used to, but hopefully…"

"Who knows?" Santos interjected. "Once he's there, it won't take long for him to find his bearings again, maybe even find his mama again, too, if he's…"

He left the rest of the sentence floating in mid-air. Both he and Willie often wondered how the two eagles had been split up—maybe something traumatic had happened, and only Wings had survived—but, neither man expressed his fears out loud.

It seemed just a flicker of time before Wings was pacing the cage constantly, opening his wings every time the latch was released for his feeding. There was no denying his readiness. Wings was yearning to be free.

Early in the morning on the big day, Dr. Mueller tagged the young eagle's leg for identification so they could track him wherever he went—and whatever might happen.

Clenching his teeth, Santos gripped the tether mount. He ran his trembling fingers along the cable that went from it to Wings' other leg. With uncanny awareness, the eagle leaned forward, obviously prepared for take-off. Willie, watching from the outside of the cage, felt his stomach tighten. He wondered how well Wings would ride in the truck. They weren't taking any chances. He would be riding in the cab with them, a cloth draped over his head to calm him until they were ready for release.

"Quite the threesome," chuckled Dr. Mueller, escorting them out the back door. "Let me know how it goes. Good luck, Wings." His voice sounded higher than usual, as he turned and ducked back inside, not waiting to see them off.

Santos and Willie stood for a quiet moment, trying to quell their emotions, working up their courage. The ocean blew them a warm breeze, stinging their nostrils with the strong odor of sea life. In harmony, they breathed in deeply, taking it all in. Wings struggled against his tether, straining toward the ocean. The two men seemed to get the same idea at once, but it was Santos who put it into words, "Long as he's secured, we might as well let him get some exercise, maybe calm him down for the trip."

Wings was in the air before the drape was off, full throttle, lifting his powerful engine up as if he'd never been grounded. Straight toward the ocean, he pulled Santos in tow.

"Willie, quick, grab my arm! Is he okay? Should we crank him back in?"

"He's doin' great," huffed Willie, jogging beside him. "Careful, there's a curb. He's headin' for the beach."

"The beach? Or the ocean?" shouted Santos. "You think he could pull us out there? Maybe you better grab on and help. I don' know, you think he could handle such a big job?"

"I don't know either, but I think he's tryin' to tell us we were about to go in the wrong direction. Somebody musta told him, you can't go back!"

Suddenly, the line went slack. Santos's face fell. "What happened?"

"Maybe it's too much for him, after all. He just landed on a big rock on the beach. Either he's tryin' to get his second wind or he's plumb outa wind. Think maybe we're kinda pushin' it?"

Santos didn't answer as he ran his free hand along the wire, hastily working his way down the bank of boulders toward the lone one on the beach, where he knew Wings would be. Willie held a firm grip on his friend's elbow, trying to help, though his own stocky legs were the ones that had to stretch beyond comfort. He stumbled more than once.

"Shhhh." Santos motioned Willie to stay back and stepped slowly forward. The eagle rustled his feathers, opening his wings at an angle, just enough to raise himself about a foot from the boulder. Sensing his angst, Santos sat down right where he was in the sand, facing the eagle, the boulder, and the sea. "Shhh. There, there, Wings. Are you tryin' to tell us somethin'?"

The boulder's pores were open wide, absorbing and reflecting their energies, just as he had with the sun's rays on the mountain. He was truly in his element now, completely fulfilled, as he gave everything he had to the two figures leaning on him.

"There's somethin' about that rock," said Willie, who'd been watching the whole scene. "You didn't dump any down here, did you, when you brought those loads from the mountain?"

Santos reached out and worked his ungloved hand all across the smooth, damp surface of the boulder, around to the sharp point that had broken off, the open crack down its middle. "This is the one I tol' you about, the one where I was sitting when heaven dropped Wings in my lap," he exclaimed. "That is all I know. Somethin' seems to draw him toward it. Almost like it's his home, and he keeps comin' back."

"What's goin' on, how'd he get so high up there?" Willie hollered from up on the jetty, about to jump down.

"I'm sorry, friend, he made me do it. He's on his way to wherever he belongs now."

"But…" Almost frantically, Willie raced out to the end of the jetty, tearing the wrapper off the trout as he made his way. An unlikely cowboy full of faith, he raised the smelly silver trophy and swung it round and round above his head, like the lasso he'd learned to throw as a kid on the ranch. A flash of a memory raced through his mind. He'd forgotten his dad had taught him how to use a lasso.

To his amazement, Wings angled sharply, tipped his broadly spread wings , and banked into a wide circle. Mouth open, Willie watched as he flew right at him, lower, closer. Things like this never happened to him! But he flung the fish up toward Wings anyway. The trajectory was high and long. Skillfully thrown, the silvery morsel slid back down, right into the eagle's path. Wings plucked his gift effortlessly out of the air and dive-bombed straight toward Willie, as if paying polite homage. Then he swooped upward, talons full and angled southwest along the coast, until he became just a dot in Willie's eye and was gone.

"Yahoo!" he yelped, almost losing his balance as he threw his arms into the air and jumped around. "I wish you coulda seen that, Santos!"

"I did, Willie. I saw it all."

Willie knew what he meant. Crumpling the fish wrap, he climbed down from the jetty, found a trash can, and rinsed his hands in the shallow pools around the eagles' boulder. "He sure seemed to know where he was headin'. You think it's that island you came through on?"

Santos reached a hand out from the perch he'd claimed on top of the boulder. Willie grabbed on, just as he had on the mountain, and allowed himself to be hoisted up next to his friend.

"Yes, I believe he follows his mama there now. I bet she has been there before. I think she must have been tryin' to lead him there for the winter when he got sidetracked, maybe by the storm—who knows? Anyway, let us hope she still survives."

"Yeah, who knows?" Willie hoped aloud. "Maybe she found herself another mate!"

"An' someday, Wings will find the mate as well." Santos smiled and allowed his thoughts to drift off. He could see himself riding the airwaves at the eagles' side, arms stretched as wide as their wings. Then, he was back at the island, startled awake by a beautiful eagle buzzing his hiding place so close it almost scraped his head. Grinning broadly into the wind, he came to the desired conclusion and dared to say it out loud. "You know? I've had this gut feeling all along that our paths have crossed before, theirs and mine. Maybe Wings' mama or papa was the one I told you about that woke me up that mornin'. Man, what an awesome moment it was, that day!"

At first, Willie thought the odds were slim, but this whole episode had shown him only too well what he now admitted aloud. "You never know! Who would have guessed we would wind up sittin' here on their rock like this, right where they used to sit on the mountain. And Wings actually came in to put his claim on it again, like he needed to let everyone know it's still theirs. And for you to find him, and their mountain roost! Wow. Sure does seem to be a connection of some sort."

"*Throne!*" the boulder wanted to shout. Nevertheless. He still swelled inside, absorbing the depth of wonder, emanating his own joyful energies. The eagles and all those before them were part of him now. As were the turtles and the little girl and the small rock with magical powers, now these two men, sitting atop him as if they knew it too. They sat there together as night settled in. Willie didn't want to break the spell, and he didn't know when he'd really, truly seen the stars and the moon on the ocean.

Santos admired them, too, in his mind's eye. He watched the lion of courage leap across the black velvet sky, the golden path that shimmered over the ocean for Marcella from the horizon to the boulder. A bronze-skinned princess with flowing hair, Marcella danced over it effortlessly all the way, right into his arms, and he folded them around her, and she kissed his wet cheeks and then moved up to his eyes.

Time stood hushed and unmoving, constant, yet changing, beginning and ending, in the whisk of each moment. All night, the waves whispered, whooshed, whispered, whooshed, *"Forever, forever, forever!"* Each separate piece was forever alone, yet forever entwined.

The sounds of dawn woke Willie first; he'd never been so aware of the world waking to so much celebration, of so many different songs, all the noise of life bustling about beginning to search for daily bread. Forcing himself to break the spell, he announced loudly enough to stir Santos, "Guess we'd better get on the road to work!"

"This is to be my work now," Santos announced in a soft, husky voice. He felt so refreshed, so alive all of a sudden, it was as if he'd been in a trance for many years and was just coming out of it into a brand new existence. During the night, a seed had been planted in his imagination, had taken root, and was already in full bloom in his mind's eye.

He jumped up and grabbed Willie's shoulders. "I have figured it out, Willie. All of it! God has talked to me through the night, as I sat here, right on this sand! My work is here! This is what I must do! You go to the mountain without me, as you must do, too! But will you help a cause once again, my friend, and bring back some things I will need?"

Willie squinted at Santos in the bright morning sun. "I don't know why I sorta thought things might settle down some now, with Wings on his way again. Is there any chance of slowin' down that busy mind of yours for just a day or two, just long enough for me to get used to things? What do you want to do now, learn to fly?"

Santos grinned at him, teeth gleaming white across at least half his tanned face as he moved closer, lowering his voice to a level that conveyed the utmost importance of his words. Willie leaned in, despite himself, and listened with rapt attention to yet another crazy Santos scheme. He was nodding in stunned compliance before he knew it. This one was really against his better judgment. But he knew there was no stopping Santos when he got an idea in his head. Willie would do what he could to help, as usual. Somehow, things always turned out okay.

That night, he submerged his exhaustion from little sleep and a long day's labor to go in search of his friend's requests, grabbing first what he could from the site, when no one was looking. He thought Santos might get in trouble with this one. Maybe he would too for aiding and abetting. Who could say why he went on the long hunt anyway, asking around, following leads, driving for hours until he'd checked off the whole list and a lop-sided gunny sack clanked around in the back of the truck? He wouldn't have missed a second of their crazy adventures so far. Why start doubting now, after seeing Santos grin again, and having that giant prince of a bird come back to him, Willie, to accept his parting gift and tip him a winged good-bye? He wouldn't have missed it for the world. Seemed like everything was really meant to happen just the way it had.

When Santos wasn't in his apartment, Willie knew he'd find him down on the beach by the boulder. Stepping up behind him, he touched his shoulder and laid the gunny sack of tools on the sand next to him. "They're all here, Santos, everything you asked for. I'll come back and check on you in a coupla days, but I gotta go now. You gotta do what you gotta do, but I can't be a part of this one, 'cause I can't afford to lose my job...or land in jail!"

Santos remained transfixed on the sand, still facing the ocean, seeing whatever he saw. He reached over, clutched the bag a minute, then raised his hand to wave Willie off. "I understan," he said. "And I am grateful. You will be glad too, I think."

"Okay," said Willie, retreating nervously.

"See you soon, Willie?"

"Yeah, I'll be by in a few days, check how you're doin'," Willie hollered over his shoulder.

241

43

Santos and the boulder waited for hours, enjoying the last ebb and flow of human sounds—the low hum of secrets being told, the splashing, running and bouncing, laughter and squeals, the creaking of chairs and umbrellas—until they all grew fainter, less frequent, and finally receded. Santos had been touching the boulder throughout the day, leaning on it with arms outstretched in giant hugs and running his hands across its smoothed surface under, around, trying to memorize the entire breadth of the granite shape, all its tiny bumps and its jagged point and deep crevice.

The boulder welcomed the man's caresses, aware that the eagle would not return, that he and the man and the ocean were right where they were meant to be, and all they were meant to be, at that very moment. Vibrant energy waves bounced between them and danced all around them before charging upward and outward, toward the distant horizon.

Dusk faded. Darkness took over. Only the ocean's rhythmic whispers and roars permeated the damp night air. The man placed a sharp instrument against the boulder's granite and held it there firmly for a long time, not moving. Then, taking a deep breath, he raised his other arm and began to pound.

The boulder winced. Something sharp was digging into him! Wrought by the same man? How could this be, such injury in the midst of the boulder's awakening, wrought by one he had grown to trust, one who had emanated such joy and caring? Was reward to be so brief? Again, the blow came, piercing into his granite. Violent change again caused by this man? Why? For what purpose? Revenge? All the boulder's hard-earned discoveries, the joyful awareness, the open acceptance began to disintegrate in the face of the new threat to his existence. Worst of all was what seemed like betrayal of the trust he had allowed himself to develop.

Once again, the eagles' throne found himself crying out toward the universe to whatever forces had made him, *"Surely, this was not meant to be! Stop him!"*

But the blows continued. He knew he shouldn't have let his guard down—especially not to one who had wrought such havoc before! Santos raised the mallet repeatedly, hammering the chisel into the boulder's surface. Furtively, the eagles' boulder began reclosing his pores. This would be the last time he would have to retreat. Now and forevermore, he would make his surface impenetrable—especially to the man and his weapons! Never again would he allow himself to be so vulnerable!

"Easy, my friend," Santos whispered, as if he sensed the boulder's struggles. "I am here to help you become even more beautiful than you already are! We are in this together, you and I, as I now know we have been from the beginning. I believe you will like what we make of you!"

In art class during his youth, Santos had learned how to shape a small rock into an awkward-looking dog. His mother still displayed it on a shelf on the dingy kitchen wall. Last night, sitting with Willie here by the boulder, right in the center of the vacuum Wings had left behind, he had slowly seen the obvious, wonderful truth. Everything he had done before, from the first art classes, to risking death for a life of freedom, to seeking in faith the fulfillment of his purpose, to backbreaking roadwork and cutting through mountains with tears streaming down his face, to feeling love and finding friendship with a bird and an unlikely man, to moving boulders, falling on them—even his limited vision, which he had hated so—had all been working together all this time, while he, completely unaware, had been building his knowledge, his senses, and his gifts. Now they had all come together, leading to this very significant moment. What's more, he knew this was not the end—only God knew where this moment would lead! Santos only had to do his part, and the rest would come.

And so, Santos toiled as he knew in his heart he was meant to do, letting his feelings and his faith lead his hands. Unaware of the boulder's defiance, he worked until he had to rest and stopped just long enough to wipe the sweat from his tanned face with one arm while he ran his other hand across the boulder's surface. Each time, he fully expected to feel at least some small dent.

But the boulder continued to resist. *More beautiful? What could the man possibly mean?* He, the eagles' boulder, had already been declared a star of the sand by the voice of the rock in the wind! He was the eagles' boulder, flecked with gold to catch the sun's rays! Hadn't he already been shaped just as he was meant to be by the forces that had made him? Wasn't he still being shaped by them? Hadn't that knowledge been part of his new understanding?

Suddenly, the chisel slid down the side of the boulder's granite, forming a long gash. "Aaaayyyy!" cried Santos. "How did it slip like that? I had good pressure on it! When did this rock get so hard?" Frowning, he ran his fingers all along the mar, down and up, back down again. He couldn't afford many mistakes like this. How would he hide it?

Seemingly from nowhere, a clear picture came into his mind, a vision in complete detail. "Ahhhaa! What was I thinking?" Santos laughed aloud. "This was also meant to be, of course! I will not only let it be just as it is! I will give it company!"

Meant to be? The man's exclamation floated lightly into the air and then drifted down with skillful aim right into the few pores that had not yet closed on the boulder. Immediately, the boulder was reminded of the small rock's admonition: *"You are fighting yourself. By defying the forces that shape your existence, you are not only fighting that which you are, at any given moment. You prevent that which you are meant to become…"*

But this was just a man with a tool, an instrument of—— Bright new enlightenment dawned once more, as the boulder reckoned again with the truth. Even as Santos chiseled pieces of him into the sand, he was still growing… if he would just let go and allow it to happen! At every moment, he would be everything he was meant to be!

And so it was that the big lopsided hunk of the mountain mother uttered a sigh of surrender to all the forces of the universe and leaned willingly into the destiny that he and this man would share. Once and for all, he allowed all his pores to open wide. He yielded to whatever would come; however, the forces wanted to shape him, whatever he was meant to be. How grand it felt!

Santos too felt relief, as his toil suddenly grew easier, results came more quickly. He couldn't explain the uncanny difference. It almost seemed as if this work of art was a joint effort, not just Santos working God's inspiration. Sometimes Santos could swear the boulder knew exactly what was taking place and was doing its part too, giving of itself freely to the purpose. There was no doubt in Santos' mind that he was finally beginning to fulfill some portion of his own purpose. Even if no one ever saw it—if he himself never saw it—this was something he must do, for the eagles, the boulder, the mountain—for every living thing that ever longed for freedom.

All through the night, Santos worked the chisel and mallet as if in a trance, hacking and chipping off pieces of the boulder's existence, letting them fall where they may in the sand, muffling the noise with his shirt folded over the mallet until the sun peeked through the darkness and began the climb, casting its brilliant gleam onto them both. The faded remnants of a red stain had been scattered like insignificant particles of dust into the sand. Feeling a little like Cinderella, Santos hustled up the bank and home to wash up, rest, and fuel up to renew his energy. The boulder knew the man would return. And so he did, for many nights, as the same drama unfolded and replayed until a brand new boulder began to take form.

Willie made a point of staying away—he knew what was on the list: a rasp, a riffler, a file, a mallet, a chisel, emery cloth. There was no changing his friend's mind, he knew by now, but he'd offered a few warnings, just to be safe. "I'm not sure what you're up to, you crazy Cuban. But I think I should warn you, with you not bein' a full citizen yet and all, just in case you don't know it yet, you could get in a whole lot of trouble, if you were to happen to deface public property. They could even send you back to Cuba! I'd hate to think of what might happen to you back there, a returning escapee."

"What makes you say those things?" Santos had shot back indignantly, "Do you not see I am sculpturin' what I hope will be a thing of beauty? I have no intent to deface anythin'! I think the authorities will see that too."

"Yeah, but it's kind of tough for the guys wearin' a badge to look the other way when a law's bein' broken. You gotta be prepared for that!"

"Thank you, Willie, I am prepared, just in case. Anyhow, I cannot refuse to do what I believe I am meant to do! You know it too, you crazy redneck! If there is trouble, I will face it then, and you need have no part of it or me… although you will always be my friend, and I, yours! And you know I am grateful for how you have helped make it possible and will never speak of it."

Willie hadn't objected out loud any more. He'd just kept quiet altogether, not letting anyone else know what was going on. That was the best he could do, along with offering up steady prayers that his good buddy wouldn't wind up in jail.

"Yeah, I see him now and then. He's doin' okay, considerin'," he'd toss out casually when one of the guys asked about Santos.

Who was he to question Santos, anyway, after everything they'd been through together? Santos was probably right, he was doing what he was meant to do. Willie was just too chicken to get more involved, and he really didn't know how to help, anyway, even if he wanted to. He didn't feel driven by some mysterious purpose, like Santos. He had no special gifts or ambitions. All he wanted to do was just live the rest of his life, maybe learn a few more things along the way, but he doubted he had any special role to play. He sure was enjoying it all a lot more now. He'd never forget the look on his dad's face when the door had opened and there'd stood Willie. He'd never seen him look like that, all melty and thankful. Of course, he'd masked his feelings mighty quick. He hadn't looked so good, and they'd both been surprised Willie cared so much. So did his dad, it turned out. They'd even sort of hugged each other.

Willie knew darned well he would never have gone if he hadn't learned a few things about life from the big Cuban dope. He felt so good about it all, he finally convinced Santos to give in, too, and write his whole sad story in a letter to Marcella and his family. Willie felt real good about that.

Marcella had sent swift reassurance of her undying love and, best of all, now that they knew where he was, they might even get a real chance to join him! It was a big to-do lately—news everywhere—out of the blue, Castro was letting a lot of Cubans just come on over. They could board a "freedom boat" if they had family here, and if they could find sufficient work to survive long enough once they'd added their names to the list. Sometimes it took years, but it was a chance.

Santos had made them promise they would come for themselves and not for him.

"If you can find your way here, you can make your way here," he had scrawled. "It will not be easy, you know. But here in America, the spirit is free to soar like the eagles, if only you will allow it to! Here we are free to be and become all that God intends for us, as long as we remain open and are willing to work hard, try once, and then again, and try again until it works. I have learned that even when injury causes us to feel that we are less, we are more. Come soon and find out for yourselves. With all my love, Santos."

Folding the letter carefully, he'd kissed it and stuffed it into an envelope, amazed at the ease with which he'd finally completed the task with little vision. His fingers had gained some of the vision his eyes had lost.

"I'm proud of you, my friend," Willie had said, taking the letter from his outstretched hand. "Guess I'll go find your secret connection now."

"What would I do without you, Willie?" Santos had shouted after him.

Willie hadn't turned back around for fear he might've choked up. "Hey, man, I'm happy to play my part!"

He'd left Santos grinning again, sitting on the sofa, far from alone.

44

The stubborn Cuban had been in jail two full days and one-and-a-half nights before Willie learned of his arrest. The boulder's changing shape had become so obvious that people were noticing it, going back for a second look, walking all around it, reaching out to touch it to see if it was real and really a boulder. They were telling their friends, who would just have to see for themselves. Some claimed it was a Styrofoam trick, a stage prop, or just a playground toy. Others delighted in the mystery. "Maybe the water is doing it! Maybe the waves just kept washing over it, year after year, until it just happened to start looking like a giant bird! Just one of nature's coincidences."

Eventually, the lifeguards had had to go to the harbor police. There was no denying it, or trying to ignore what was happening anymore. That night, they'd lain in wait together behind the mountain's boulders up on the jetty. It had been all too easy to make their move as soon as Santos had set the bag of tools on the sand and pulled out the riffler to resume his work.

They saw no real harm in what he was doing and had told him so. "You just didn't leave us a whole lot of choice!" they'd complained. "You could've been sneakier, so it wasn't so obvious. There are laws, man, and we're bound to enforce them! You can't just do that. You can't mess with our protected nature and expect us not to interfere. Think of the mess we'd have if everyone decided to follow their fancy."

The handcuffs hadn't really been necessary. Still they'd put his hands behind his back and clamped them on. "I understan' your position," Santos had stated, shuffling between them, listening to the jangle of their keys. "I even respect your position. But I would like to explain how it all came about, and what I am trying to accomplish."

"You know what, man? Tellin' us won't do any good."

"You'll have your chance to tell it to the judge," the desk warden had added, pushing Santos forward gently. Then he'd slammed the cell door behind him, turned the key in the lock and gone back to his desk. A shudder had raced through Santos, so strong it had almost knocked him off his feet. He might have heard those sounds in Cuba and never emerged again! Despite Willie's warnings, he'd never imagined he would hear them here. Moaning aloud, he'd backed up to a wooden bench against the cold concrete wall and bent over to rest his head in his hands. His palms had felt rough and dry against the clammy skin on his face.

"Ayyyy, what now?" he had moaned. "Santos, you have done it now! You can take the man out of Cuba! But you can't take Cuba out of the man!"

Steady drips of perspiration from his forehead had splashed on to the concrete floor. This fear was unnatural! He was in America! Deep down, he knew it. How could he let his emotions get the best of him like this? He just knew that help would come! His purpose still awaited its completion. Nothing could really happen to him, could it, at least until he'd completed his work? Why couldn't he slow the beating in his chest? What would happen to the boulder? Would they try to move it, climb on it, ruin the work he had started? Would he be allowed to go back and finish? How long would he have to be here?

Feeling completely desperate, Santos fell to his knees on the hard concrete floor and bowed his head. "Please, God, if you want that I should do this. Is it okay for you to help pretty soon now?"

45

The road crew had come in off the job full of dust to grab a cool drink and some lunch when Hank snorted at them from behind the newspaper, peering over the top rim of his glasses, "What'll that crazy eagle lover do next?"

Willie rushed with the rest of the guys to cluster behind Hank's chair, leaning forward to read over his shoulder. In the lower right corner of the front page was a clear picture of the eagles' boulder in his current state of becoming a big granite eagle on the sand. "Errant Artist Carves His Way INTO Jail" read the headline.

Hank jumped to his feet, wadding the paper into a bundle under his arm. "Come on, guys, looks like our buddy needs some help. Let's go get him out."

For a minute, Willie stood with his mouth open. Who'd have thought that snarly old Hank would be the one to beat him to the punch and lead the charge? Seemed like Santos had worked his magic on them all.

"So, how long have you known about this one, Willie?" Hank shot over his shoulder as he leaped up behind the wheel and all eight of the other men headed for the bed of the nearest dump truck. Willie managed not to answer, working his legs as fast as he could to pile in with the rest, beating Sammy to the last spot in the back. Sammy had barely climbed up into the cab when Hank squealed out, wasting no time. Shards of rock bounced around on the metal, and there was no getting comfortable. *But first things first*, thought Willie. *Avoid being grilled by Hank, and rescue Santos.* He leaned his head back and watched the clouds race along overhead. He was proud to belong to this cavalry!

"That'll be two-hundred-dollars bail, and he needs to sign right here, stating he won't deface public property any more," said the warden, looking down at his papers as he offered up a pen.

"You come here for me?" Santos sang out again and again, gripping the bars in front of him. "That crazy, blind immigrant who stirs up the trouble, you come here for me?" He could hardly contain his joy or his gratitude.

"We come here for *us!*" shouted Hank. "We're *all* immigrants, every darned one of us! And there ain't a human being alive who ain't at least a little bit blind. Especially these jailers!"

"You'll find yourself behind bars too if you don't watch your mouth," said the warden.

"Come on, Santos, let's get you outa here," said Willie. "We took up a collection. All you gotta do is sign right here, promising not to deface protected public property any more, and they'll let you out without any charges."

"But I can't do that! Willie, you know that I cannot!" Santos shook his head no with extreme moves from side to side. Backing up, he sat down on the bench again and kept shaking his head to leave no doubt. "It is very tempting, and you are all very good. Believe me, I am grateful, and I want out of here so much you will never know how much! But it would be very bad for me to sign that. I must continue with my work. It is my destiny!"

"You gotta be kiddin'!" yelled Hank. "You mean we've come all this way to help, and you won't even..."

"If he signed, he wouldn't be Santos," Willie boldly interrupted in a low, matter-of-fact voice. "Sure woulda been a dull, dumb job without that stubbornness of his."

"Yeah, and his idealism," chimed Andy. "Standin' up for your beliefs, I call that downright American!"

Santos tossed his head back, laughing out loud, consumed with joy. The men smiled broadly at him, shrugged their shoulders, and followed Hank outside in single file.

"Guess they gave up on you," said the warden. "Guess you're gonna have to face the music or your limitations, like the rest of us if you ever wanna get outa here! Come on, don't make me have to be a bad guy here!"

Santos leaned back against the wall, folding his arms across his chest, enjoying the sudden calm that was washing over him. "I know I must obey the law," he stated firmly. "But where does it say a man cannot complete a design that God has begun, not only on the boulder, but on me? Life is not about your limitations, but what you are meant…"

His voice trailed off, as he heard shouts from outside and recognized the raised voices of Willie and Al and Pete and Andy, Sammy and Kevin and Harry in unison. "Free Santos! Sand Harbor Police unfair! Make them free the freedom artist!" They marched in a circle, holding up signs with scrawled sketches of birds on wing and bold letters. "Free the man who freed the eagles!"

Santos didn't need to see them. The scene was clear in his mind. He smiled softly and bowed his head.

Curious crowds began to gather. One by one, in groups and pairs and all alone, they made their way down to the beach, bound to see for themselves, as humans are inclined to do. "Would you look at that!" they marveled aloud. "When did that guy manage to do all this? Sure looks good to me! Wow! Why, it's an eagle, you can see it as plain as the nose on your face! And they say he can't even see the nose on his own face, he's so blind! Wow. It's already an accomplishment of rare beauty, if you ask me!"

The boulder began to glow with pride. He had heard it himself—a thing of beauty, once again, as he was always meant to be! The sun beamed down on him, magnifying the sparkle of the gold flecks on his surface even more. "Wow! And he's not even finished yet! Why don't they let him finish?" Held together by a common purpose, the growing crowd of individuals moved toward the jail and joined the workers in noisy protest.

Before night moved in, reporters arrived with bright lights and eager cameras. They took pictures of Santos, of the men with their signs, of the growing crowd. They captured the foreboding threat of the tiny Sand Harbor Police Station sign. The stories spread themselves in brash condemnation of Santos' plight and the ominous, pervasive threat to freedom. A bigger photo had moved to the top of the page now, not just in the Sand Harbor Press, but in almost every paper across the nation. There it was, a lone boulder on the beach, or, was it an eagle? The picture by the story clearly showed how the boulder's jagged point had been rounded and shaped like Mama Eagle's beak, strong and foreboding. Its middle formed its breast, with deep grooves stretching out away from it toward feathered edges, already discernible. One editor got creative and gave it a caption that said it all, without realizing the perfect fit made by the headline: Wings.

46

Immigrant Escapes Communism—Protects Freedom and Life for Eagles—and Loses His Own Freedom: Is This America? Marcella read it all aloud to Santos' mama' and papa' in English, her voice in a husky whisper, as loudly as she dared. The American paper had somehow found its way into her hands. Clutching it to her bosom under her blouse, both nervous and excited, she'd rushed to see them as soon as she'd felt reasonably sure no one was looking. They huddled tightly together around the small wooden table Santos himself had carved, as if to shut out the dangers around them and it. Mama ran her hand reverently in circles over the top, fingering the nicks carved into it over the years of their lives in this little house. All their eyes were damp as emotions passed between them, zigzagging from pride to excitement, to shock and disappointment, as well as worry for Santos and themselves. They still hadn't received any clearance to board a ship.

"Even if we still could, after this," rasped Manuel. "Do we really still want to? How could all this have happened in America? Perhaps it is no better than Cuba, after all!"

His wife reached out and slapped his shoulder with the back of her worn hand. "You know it is! Would you ever read something like this in *Libre Cuba*? No, no, it is Santos! Leave it to Santos, he is one stubborn boy! I will have to get there now and pound some sense back into that wooden head of his!" Jumping up to control her emotions, she tried to wipe the sudden longing out from her eyes with her apron.

Marcella wrung her hands and smiled, moved by the depth of their obvious affection. "This is why he did not come, or write, or send for us, as we'd planned," she said wistfully. Her chin trembled. Both she and Mama' broke down at the same moment, sobbing together. Mama' felt only pain for her son. Marcella wept, too, for his pain. But it was mixed with relief. And guilt for that.

"Somehow," she murmured longingly, "we must go to him ourselves."

Both his parents snapped their heads toward her, eyes bulging in surprise and disbelief.

Mama' was the first to come to the same conclusion, "Yes!" she cried.

"You are both loco!" snapped Papa'. "How we do this now, when Santos cannot help us get there from here?"

"How we *not* go to *him*?" snapped Mama'. "He needs us more than ever, now!"

"Shhhh!" Papa' suddenly cautioned, slapping his whole hand over his mouth. They all snapped to attention, froze like statues. A jeep had screeched to a stop just outside. Not one, but two car doors opened and slammed shut. Loud footsteps echoed on the cobblestones just outside the house. The three small figures inside seemed to shrink even more as they all held their breath.

47

"N o!" shouted Santos, jumping up from the shelf-like chair built into the wall of his cell.

Willie, who had beamed as he'd read the headline to him, frowned in puzzlement. At the very least, he'd expected Santos to match his excitement. "What, you don't like a little publicity? You don't think this'll help us get you outa there and let you finish what you started?"

"You don' know Castro!" Santos had shot back. "He is now aware where he was not before! I have been the fool! Now *he* has been made the fool, and I am the cause. Santos Gonzales has embarrassed the Maximum Leader! He has become the big whale instead of the little minnow. I have made the big show of how I wanted to get away from the great society of Castro! And did!"

Santos paced with long strides, wringing his hands one minute, wiping his forehead the next. His black hair glistened with sweat. "No. He will not stand for being made the fool. Mark my word, Castro will strike back."

He stopped in his tracks and spun toward Willie, grabbing his shoulders imploringly. "I must go right away."

"What? Go where?"

"Please, Willie. Summon the warden. I will sign the paper. I know now what I must do. Every minute counts! Please hurry!"

48

The very next night, two small groups on opposite shores moved stealthily, words muffled and sparse. Her wet cheeks squeezed tightly between those of her own parents, Marcella had hugged them good-bye, assuring herself as well as them that she would be able to send for them soon, and they would see each other again very soon, in better times.

They had shaken their heads resignedly. "It is too late for us. Go and make a good life for yourself. That means more to us than our own freedom."

Grasping the bread that her mother had thrust into her hands, she'd forced her body out the door to join Santos' parents in the deep woods outside of town, where they were waiting, having already bid a tearful good-bye to the little hut where Santos had been raised. They'd decided they should go separately through the dark streets to raise less suspicion. The smaller the group, the less noise and attention.

"It must be now!" was all Marcella had scribbled just the day before, when they had held their breath after reading the American paper, waiting for the footsteps to come from the jeep to the door, the demanding knock that could change their lives forever. They had only had to face their own fears that night. But they could not afford to wait. They knew they would continue to hear the jeep every day, every night—perhaps only in intimidation but never knowing if that would be all. Their nerves could not have stood the suspense. Somehow, word would get out, someone would snitch for a bag of bananas, and they would never be allowed to leave the island.

And so, the note had been passed through familiar channels, and they could only hope it had been received by those waiting to hear from them, in time. In the middle of the night, they had gathered only enough to survive on so that no one outside immediate family circles would miss them until they had had time to escape.

Now they all breathed a sigh of relief to find their guide was there, too, at the edge of the marsh. They hadn't even known his name—only how to reach him, when the time was right. They would need to follow him through the swamp with no trails and no sense of direction in the dark of night. They hoped to make it through the hinterland and the swamp in two nights, as Santos had done. Marcella had been glad they'd agreed together that she could make the painful and dangerous land trip right behind Santos and the mysterious guide so she would know the way if they ever had to try to make it alone. Just in case. But it is so much better, to follow this trusted savior, she thought, smiling weakly up at his serious face as they all turned their bodies resolutely into the deep darkness.

The swamp was hot and wet, always with the threat of a fast-moving alligator with huge jaws that could snap a steel-like trap down upon its victim and drag him or her to a painful demise. They pulled against the quicksand-like mud with their fisherman's boots, which they'd been warned to wear. The layers of clothing they'd had to put on weighed them down, but that, too, was a necessity. Marcella listened nervously to the heavy breathing of the older couple, always alert for a sudden cry from either of them. But though meager rations through the years had weakened them physically, life in Cuba had toughened their hides as well as their resolve. Neither of them uttered the slightest whimper of self-pity throughout the dark nights of marching like soldiers toward freedom.

49

At the same time, Willie was fighting a queasy stomach, leaning against the rail beside his friend as the fishing boat churned through the choppy Caribbean waters, leaving the safety and warmth of American shores far behind. He must be getting used to Santos. He hadn't even called him crazy this time, before he'd sprung into action, scrambling to bring another of his wild ideas to fruition. Besides, Willie wouldn't have had him any other way. The whole story would probably have made the papers without him eventually. But he was the one who'd called the *Gazette News* desk to get them to the jailhouse first. Then, it was all he could do to keep the news out of the paper when they'd opened the cell door, and Santos had rushed out, a free but troubled man. He hadn't been able to change Santos' mind, of course, so he'd decided he'd better go with him. If he had to be Santos' eyes on the boat, when he'd always had to fight getting seasick, so be it. And to keep her quiet for now, he'd had to make a deal with the reporter.

The next night, they'd watched a dark shadow on the ocean grow into a sizeable vessel as it drew up before them. On a good trip, its wooden planks would be thick with mackerel or tuna or halibut, still wiggling their graceful ocean bodies awkwardly, desperately against the unforgiving wood. He couldn't help wondering if they would be swimming there too, right amongst the mackerel on the return trip.

"Willie, I beg you, stay here, right here in America. I will see you back here again soon. These fishermen know what needs to be done. They are well practiced. I want you here and waiting for us on this shore, by our boulder friend, when I return with my loved ones. This could be a dangerous journey, and I would not want anything bad to happen to you."

"That's why I'm going with you," said a distinctively familiar female voice with a Southern drawl. Santos whirled around toward the voice. A willowy shape stepped out of the shadows and moved toward them. He could hear her camera gear jingling as it hung from a strap from her leather-clad shoulder across her chest. "I figure if anything gets rough, Americans oughta know about it."

Santos let out a string of Spanish words not fit for the lady's ears, or anyone's. Waving his hands wildly toward the boat, he shouted, not even caring who might hear him,

"That is it! I go alone, just me, with these fishermen who know the way and how to do it right! Willie, now you have gone too far. You think I will let either one of you take this chance, you are the loco ones! Only Santos! Not Willie! And not Miss Gotta-Get-the-News-Out! No! I go without you both! It is a dangerous journey!"

Willie hollered back, "I'm goin' whether you like it or not!" just as a large frame jumped off the bank along the beach and strode up the gangplank toward them, drowning them both out with a shout, "Yeah, we know! That's why we're goin' along to protect you all."

Santos spun around again, this time toward a deep male voice. "Al?"

"Yeah."

Another shadow approached, announcing, "Yeah, Andy and Pete too! We figure you might need some help if the goin' gets a little rough."

Willie broke into a nervous laugh. "You guys are too much! What does Hank think of this craziness?"

"He's all for it!"

Both he and Santos whirled again, this time toward the foreman's unwavering declaration as he jumped down from the bank and strode toward them.

"Car-r-r-umba! You too?"

"Well no, I just came to let you know all these crazy guys here got my *okay*. If I didn't have to stay with the job, I'd be goin' along too." He put a hand on Santos's shoulder.

269

"But, this way you know I'm okay with them goin' along to keep you two outa trouble."

"Yeah, and he seen to it we got plenty of grub," said Al, throwing a sack over his shoulder and heading for the boat. "See ya soon, boss! You'll probably miss us more'n we'll miss you!"

"Lots o' luck gettin' that road down before we get back!" yelled Andy.

Willie put his hand in the middle of Santos' back and pushed him toward the loading platform.

"Hey, Willie, you pushin' me again? And me, I just am lettin' you? What am I comin' to?"

"On board, you measly landlubbers," called Pete from the deck. "Let's move this pack o' pirates out!"

Santos grinned broadly and leaned back against Willie's hand, letting him do the work of moving them both. "Hah! You guys are plain loco, for sure! You crazy, redneck Americans! You more than loco! You…"

"Yeah, yeah, look at the hot-blooded Cuban we hang around with!" yelled Hank as he thrust his heels down hard in the sand against the magnetic pull of the group. "Hurry back!" he felt compelled to add, tightening his throat against the tremor that fought to be heard. "I need you guys!"

He started to lean back against the boulder behind him but felt a sharp jab from what now resembled an eagle's beak. He turned around and caressed the rock's surface fondly, "You sure started somethin'," he said out loud. If he hadn't known better, he'd have sworn that rock could have spread its wings and taken off right then and there, to follow the boat full of unlikely fishermen of men, and a woman, all the way to Cuba.

50

On an island somewhere between the two shores, many large birds with white bodies and dark heads mingled in varying sizes of groups, enjoying the riches of Eagle Island. Wings and his mother had found each other easily. Now she sidled slightly away from her mate to nuzzle her grown son's neck and prick sharply at the mites on his head. "You have grown well, my son. I am glad you finally joined us here. No doubt some adventure led you astray. I am not surprised at that. But I knew you would make it."

As if to show off his highly developed skills, the young eagle leaped off the coarse river sand, streaking strong and straight, like an arrow shot from a giant's bow, up, up toward the lazy clouds. He hovered for long moments high above, as if he'd been hung up there by a hook. Spotting a trout in the river below, swimming too lazily for its own good, the eagle aimed his beak right for it, shot back to earth, and brushed across the water with ready talons. Scooping the trout up all too easily, he flew low right past his mother, then shot up again, fish in tow. She launched up after him. Seeing her coming, Wings dropped the fish toward her and looped into a backward somersault. She swooped under it, then up past it just in time to snatch it in midair. "Ahhhha! See if you can catch this!" she sang out, flying past him as she released it. They played together all afternoon like youngsters on the ground with a ball, as though they'd never left each other's side. All the while, though, deep within the young eagle's breast, a sense of uneasiness kept tugging at him. Something was pulling at him again. He fought the urge to be drawn into its magnetism as he struggled to understand.

51

As soon as the guide put his hand up to bring the small troop to a halt, Marcella, right behind him, raised her own for the others to see. They had reached the edge of the marsh, almost to the beach where the boat was supposed to come for them. Trying not to breathe too loudly, they hid shivering for the next two hours, more and more fearful that they would be left behind because someone else had the government's ear and influence. Many in the Great Society eventually learned to distrust everyone else. Their little band of friends and family only pretended disloyalty to each other and loyalty above all else to the Maximum Leader. But others did not pretend. One never knew who might betray another for some small handout or favor, or even for the gift of survival.

They crouched in silence, no one moving. Only the sounds of the woods mixed with what breathing they dared. An orange ball peeked shyly over the line of the horizon and splashed the sky with dainty pink puffs of cotton. A parrot pierced the silence with a hearty call, and even stoic Papa' jumped. They all looked at each other with wide eyes of great relief and managed to exchange wary smiles, gifts for each other, a moment of light relief.

Finally, after what seemed like hours, the guide motioned for them to stay put and stepped cautiously toward the water's edge to get a better look. If the boat didn't come soon, they would have to take their chances and sneak back. Here, they would be detected by the soldiers in daylight. In town, they would all be missed before the sun went down. The guide would be in more danger than any of them. No one knew what he did until they were ready to need him and pay him. He did what he could to survive; if he could help too, then that was good. But he must not be caught.

Signaling for them to stay put, he wrapped his legs around the trunk of a coconut tree and shimmied up its trunk for a better line of sight. The three small figures gaped up at him until their necks ached and their eyes stung from squinting in the warming sun. Mosquitoes and gnats were drawn by the sweat that began to ooze from their pores. A slap on the skin would be far too noisy. They could only swipe at them and shake their heads to try to avoid the bites. Papa' especially had to resist slapping hard at the blood-sucking monsters—the only way he could keep from it was by pretending they were undercover agents for Castro, and he wasn't about to give them the satisfaction of getting them all caught in their trap.

The sun had shown its entire face by the time the guide shimmied back down the trunk of the tree. He crept to them, grinning broadly, nodding his head vigorously. "It comes!" he mouthed.

Excitement struggled onto their weary faces as they quickly gathered their one bag each and slid down the steep bank as carefully as possible, readying themselves for boarding the boat as soon as it drew close enough for them to reach it—even if it meant plunging into the waves and swimming against its wake.

Willie had been straining forward over the rail next to Santos, his sense of optimism quarreling inside with what he feared would be reality. He'd half expected to find an empty shore and wait for hours, until they would finally have to give up and turn the ship back around without the treasure they'd come seeking. When three small figures slipping and sliding toward the water's edge materialized in the lens of his spyglass, his astonished attempt at a whisper came out in a shout, "There they are!"

He and Santos grabbed at each other in jubilation. "Where? Turn me toward them, Willie, please! I see shadows of trees, but I do not know…"

"We're aimin' right at 'em! Right there, comin' toward us!"

Santos couldn't hold back. With no warning, surprising even himself, he yanked free from Willie's grasp, climbed up on the rail, dove into the satin waves, and swam straight forward, what he hoped was just a few hundred feet to shore.

"It's Santos!" cried Marcella.

"Santos! Thank God! But what is he doing in the water, is that safe? How can he see where he's going? How will he find us?" Mama' worried aloud as she and her husband leaned on each other and watched him nervously, their feet sinking into the soggy sand.

"I will find *him*!" Marcella sang out, half laughing, as she ran splashing toward him until the water was up to her waist. She dove toward the swiftly approaching swimmer, calling out with abandon, forgetting not to shout, "Santos! You come for us! We are all here, your mama' and papa'! And me, Marcella! Here I am!" She couldn't reach the bottom by the time they fell against each other, whispering each other's names as they treaded water and kissed each other's cheeks, savoring the salty mixture of seawater and tears. After a long moment, Santos took Marcella's hands and pulled her around behind him. "Hang on!" he warned, plunging forward with her on his back.

His parents were upon him before he could stumble completely out of the water. Marcella's feet quickly dug into the sand behind him, as they both struggled to regain their balance. In an instant, eight arms were entwined, all hugging as tightly as their tired muscles could manage.

Both Mama' and Marcella reached up to pat Santos' eyes tenderly, each with one hand. "How do you see to swim right here to us?" asked Mama'.

Santos bent down and whispered in her ear, "I see more with my heart now."

"Ah, the family reunion!" The voice was loud and brittle, like a bugle waking a soldier's too brief respite from his harsh reality. "What, you think we that stupid we don' know what's happening between the two countries, one being so considerate as to send us back our pigs to squeal as they roast on the spit?"

The small group in the shallow water cringed. Instinctively, they tightened their hold on each other in mutual protection.

"What have I brought you to?" cried Santos.

"It is a trap!" shouted Papa'. Mama' and Marcella squeezed their eyes shut, trying to close out the terrible fear that gripped them. Were they about to be shot? Tortured? Were they going to march Santos before a jeering crowd and then stand him before a firing squad? Would the rest of them be thrown into cold dark cells, never again to see the light for the rest of their lives?

As three uniformed men marched up to surround them, the guide tried to slink back into the brush, hoping they hadn't seen him.

"You!" barked the tallest soldier, waving a pistol toward him and motioning him to move into the huddle. "You, we can hang like a pig to roast on the fire until you are nothing but ashes, for you are the traitor that brought these civilians here to try to escape our beloved country. Why would you

278

do that? Why would any of you want to run from your mother country?"

The one with the thickest beard snorted through his cigar, "No one would mourn for you. No one cares about traitors!"

"But the rest of you!" a younger man with broad shoulders and a very black moustache and beard that mirrored Castro's bellowed, "You, blind eagle man, Meester Artiste, you and your beloved, and your mama' and papa'— all of you we will have to reeducate for the change of the headlines in the American paper!"

"Now you will paint and carve your way to true fame, Santos!" the man with the fat cigar chimed in. He rolled the cigar with his tongue to the corner of his mouth for emphasis and looked Marcella up and down mockingly. "Now the famous artiste will carve the statue of our Maximum Leader. You carve the animals so good you will place him atop his beautiful horse—and there he will be for all the world to see, in Havana's town square."

"And we will take your picture by it, when you have completed your masterpiece. This we will send to the American paper so they know the truth of your loyalty!" sneered the tall captain, brandishing his pistol. "Then you will be famous in both Cuba and America. And as long as you are famous...and loyal to your heritage...you will live, Mr. Eagle Man! And so will these others, your lover... your familia!"

"Eeeeeeaahh!"

Just as he finished his sentence, leaning back in a boastful, full-chested pose, a shrill shreek filled the air, shot from the feathered torpedo that was streaking out of the blue above right toward his head.

"What the....?" The captain jerked his gaze up toward the threatening noise. "What kind of bird is that?" he demanded, pointing his pistol right at Wings, who was aiming right for his eyes.

Zing! The gun went flying out of his hand before he could pull the trigger.

"Owwww!"

He grabbed his hand in pain and whirled toward the beach just as Wings hit his mark, knocking his hat to the ground and leaving a long gash across the top of his head.

"Owwwww!"

"Where'd that come from?"

"I don' know, but I will find out! Where did that crazy bird come from?"

Zing! Just as he finished the sentence, half the bearded one's cigar was shot away, and he was left dazed, staring down cross-eyed at its brown stub. Al and Willie climbed up over the bank they'd swum to as soon as they'd seen the soldiers. "Hold it right there, Amigo," warned Willie, cocking his rifle again as he jogged toward them, throwing caution to the wind. "I'd drop all them there weapons, if I's you'ns."

"What? More loco fools? Fools from America, land of the capitalistic pigs?" sputtered the one with the Castro-like beard. "You think you come here so easy to come and then go? To escape back away?"

"Your little bitty army will not survive," moaned the captain, grasping his hand, then rubbing his head, not sure which pain to rub first. "Do you not know of the Cuban navy? It is mighty, and you will be hunted down as soon as you leave. They are on the lookout for you. We only let you come so close to our shore so you could bring the Cuban citizen back to his homeland. What, you add an attack bird to your pitiful brigade, you can't handle the battle yourself?"

Suddenly, the sky above them went dark. Like a huge cloud, a mass of eagles screamed shrill warnings. Three mighty birds broke from the crowd and aimed straight toward them like lightning bolts.

"Aeeeee! You get that one! I'll go for the short one!" Mama Eagle called to her mate, as she zoomed down to join Wings. This was like old times! Both eagles aimed right for the soldiers' heads, screeching a warning just before they hit their targets. The men grabbed at their faces and reeled backward, trying to protect themselves against the onslaught.

"What kind of birds are those? Is it the eagle? Cuba has no eagles! They do not inhabit our land!"

"They do now!" laughed Pete, who'd come in behind his friends and was frisking each of the guards, just in case. "Looks like we brought a whole army of 'em!"

Suddenly, the sky was filled with huge birds, a cloud of black and white, a few still all brown, like Wings, crisscrossing, zooming down in threatening grazes over the Cuban soldiers' heads.

Santos watched the thrashing shadows in happy amazement, laughing out loud, "Wings! Is Mama Eagle here, too? You have come to our rescue?"

"Yeah, and a whole mess more came with 'em!" shouted Willie. "You are one enchanted dude, my friend!"

"Enchanted!" cried the Castro-bearded soldier, rubbing at the scratches on his face. "It is the magic. The witch doctor! The brujeria! He has the black magic of the brujeria, controlling the eagles of America!"

"I'll finish the tall one!" commanded Wings. "You get the other two. Eeeaah!"

Wings sped toward the captain's face, while Mama Eagle took aim at the thickly bearded one, and her mate went for the one with the short stick in his mouth. The big eagle's talons barely grazed the stunned man's lips as it flew past and grabbed what was left of the cigar. They were followed by three more eagles, then a pack of five big eagles, crisscrossing each other with threatening calls aimed at the hapless soldiers. The startled men were flailing their arms all around, trying to swat at the birds and shield their heads. They stumbled backward and fell in a heap, shaking with fear, though the most they had suffered were scratches and embarrassment.

"The eagle man really has become a witch!" screamed the captain. "The brujeria lives through him! She has touched him! Run! The eagle does not come to Cuba! The artiste has painted black magic! He commands a whole army of eagles to fly here from America! Let them all go! Let's get out of here! We must let them all go away, leave us and our shores. We are better off without them!"

As they scrambled into the jeep, the captain motioned toward the boat with a sweeping gesture. "Go! We will not say that you were here! Go back to America and take everyone with you. Stay there, you and your eagle army! We do not want your black magic here! Do not come back!" He turned the key and spun the tires of the jeep backward, then turned the wheel sharply away from their would-be prisoners.

"They do not know we had them caught," he yelled at his compadres. The others nodded and swiped at the blood on their faces, leaving traces of dirt from their sweaty palms. They would have to sneak in, somehow, and clean up.

"No one ever needs to know. They would not believe. They would laugh at us. We would be called the cowards. We will tell our superiors that no one came. We saw no one."

Watching them skid away, Willie turned his head toward the boat and grinned. Kate was hanging out over the bow of the boat, brandishing her own weapon.

"Unbelievable," she said to Andy, who'd been helping her capture the whole scene on film as it unfolded before them. "Wait 'til they see this picture splashed right across page one."

"That's the only way anyone could believe it really happened," said Pete, shaking his head back and forth. "I still don't believe it, and I seen it with my own eyes."

Santos, Marcella, Mama', and Papa' hadn't moved. Still arm in arm, they had stood their ground in the ankle-deep water. Grinning ear to ear, Santos clucked out a call to his friends, "Wings! Mama Eagle! You come back to Santos and Willie! You have come back!"

By now, most of the eagles had circled around again toward Eagle Island. They had followed Wing's promise of adventure and the plea for their help. Indeed. Such fun! So uncommon! But now they must return to the quest for survival, to life itself, to their own freedoms. Only Wings and Mama Eagle flew toward Santos, her mate hovering nearby. Dipping low in a bow of respect, they flew right by him, up, and then back several times before they swooped away, the wind from their wings caressing his face.

"Thank you! Muchas gracias!" he called after them. "It is the gift of freedom we bestow upon each other again and again! You have honored and amazed me once again!"

The eagles sang a sweet good-bye and spun off in wing formation back toward their island.

52

The waves were kind once again, as the fishing boat chugged its way back home. The storms that might have threatened the exhausted passengers at a moment's notice with giant, slashing hands and howling winds that could blow the dilapidated vessel into pieces of scrap wood, dashing its hapless humans into the depths, avoided them altogether. The boat, too, had its purpose. Somehow, it had also steered them clear of the big ships that lined the Cuban coast, always on alert for those who were foolish enough to try to leave paradise. And though they had run out of drinking water on the second day, a gentle rain had filled their cups with enough to stave off the temptation to drink the ocean's salty poison. "God protects us, coming and going!" Santos exclaimed.

By the time the refugees disembarked on the sand of the big island that was their first destination, Willie and Kate's friendship had blossomed. "You folks get cleaned up and relax awhile here on this beach," he said. "I'll see you when you get good and ready to come on. Think I'd better see the lady safely home. She's got a press pass that'll get us all on the next flight to Miami, and we gotta get back to the road buildin' while she gets this story to her editor."

He pressed American dollars into Santos' hand as he shook it. "Don't try not to take it," he said in a low voice so he wouldn't embarrass his friend. "This comes from all of us, but especially Hank, who wanted to help any way he could. Besides, I got a feelin' you'll be able to pay us all back in no time."

"Okay, I will even clean the latrine if I have to," said Santos, putting his big arms around the shoulders of Marcella, Mama', and Papa' all at once and ushering them up the beach toward the zesty waft of a juicy steak being grilled. Marveling at his strength and stamina, they leaned on him and gratefully allowed themselves to be led together toward their emancipation.

They were all dumbfounded at his announcement later, as they waited eagerly for the steaks to be served. "I realize now, I must give up the dreaming to be the artiste," he said flatly.

His three companions studied his face, searching for the smile that would reveal his tease. "Perhaps not with the brush or the chalk," Mama' offered quickly. "But now you have discovered a new…"

"What I discovered," he interrupted gently, "was based on a memory. Something dear to my heart that has come and gone. All I really accomplished was trouble. Me, in the American jail. And you, my loved ones…I almost got us all locked up in Cuba for life!"

Marcella reached out and covered his hand with her own. "What you got, Santos, was the freedom for us all. And that was all we ever wanted…freedom…and you. You will find more beauty to share with the world, in your own way, as God intended."

"But that is just it," Santos insisted. "Would God have brought us all this trouble if He truly wanted Santos to be the artiste?"

"Anything that is worth the doing," interjected Papa', "is worth the trouble. Hah! You think this is trouble? Try going back to the homeland now! Or try living through the Batista years and the Revolución! This is not trouble. So you don' see so good no more. Use the feelings more, like with the rock and the eagles. Maybe that is what God wanted from you all along."

The waitress approached with two sizzling plates on each arm. Santos, Mama', and Marcella didn't even seem to notice. They were all staring at Papa'—even Santos, who could only see the outline of his head—stunned by the old man's sudden expression of optimism and faith.

"The man of many sour words speaks sweetly and wisely tonight," said Mama', patting her husband's arm. "Ah, real food! Will our stomachs even know what to do with it?"

For the next several days, Santos discovered the little money he had would hardly spend. His fame had arrived before him. "The eagle man!" little boys called out whenever he passed. Already sympathetic toward refugees seeking freedom from tyranny, the islanders seemed highly impressed by Santos' fame and went out of their way to make him and his family as comfortable as possible.

Santos couldn't seem to touch his loved ones enough. He and Marcella spent most of their days stretched on the sand, hands reaching out to touch the ends of each others' fingers, as they had the night they'd parted so long ago on the Motherland's shores. They smiled dreamily, knowing they would not be forced to part again. "I cannot believe it," Papa' kept repeating. "Are we really here?" Sometimes they would laugh out loud at something funny without thinking, then glance warily over a shoulder, just to make sure that no one who could bring trouble had heard.

They'd all gathered in Santos' room, chattering aimlessly one late morning after breakfast, when a loud knock sounded at the closed door. Each body came to stiff attention, fighting the urge to try hiding under the bed. Was reality about to smack them between the eyes again? Had the soldiers found them again and come for them, after all?

Santos was the first to venture warily, "Who is it?"

"Well, it ain't no enemy! Open up, man, the day's gettin' away from us!"

"Hah! Willie! You old dog!" shouted Santos, reaching the door in two long strides to fling it open. "I been wonderin' how long you gonna let Santos be lazy!" They shared a quick man-hug.

"Here! Put these on and get out here, all of you! We got a boat waitin' for you out here!" Willie said as he thrust a bundle of cloth toward his friend.

"What? You don' like the way we look, like the true refugees that we are, we gotta get cleaned up just for a boat ride?"

"Not just *a* boat ride, Santos. *The* boat ride of your life! Wait 'til you board her!"

Marcella was unraveling the bundle. "Look at the fine material, Mama!" she exclaimed. "They are white, Santos! And, linen!"

Willie was beaming ear to ear. Marcella could tell something was up and nodded with exaggeration, exchanging knowing glances with him and Mama' and Papa'. "Thank you, Willie, muchas gracias! You are very kind. We will get cleaned up right away and meet you on the boat as soon as possible!"

Santos quickly surmised he was outnumbered. "Ah, it is for the woman who will be in my life from now on that I go along with this cleaning up for the trip," he announced jovially as they approached the dock. "What kind of boat is it?"

"Well, it's kind of a big one," said Willie. "For some reason, they wanted you to travel in style."

Santos looked toward him quizzically, then bowed with extended arm, ushering them toward a sleek blue-and-white yacht he could only see was a very big blob.

"It is very fancy," said Papa'. "Is everything in America big and fancy, like this?"

Santos laughed. "I don' know how fancy this is. But, no, you certainly will not find that is the case there. I must apologize already for the little room I will take you to today, and that is where we must all reside until I can save enough money from building the roads for us to have two rooms."

"We can all work," offered Mama'. "It will not all be up to you, my son."

Santos rubbed his hand over the satin finish of the railing. "One thing for sure, it is a bit more comfortable than the boats I have been on before! Hank and the gang give far too much. I don' know how I will ever repay them."

He'd barely completed his sentence before he had to brace himself against a sudden lurch forward by the powerful engine of the big yacht. They sliced through the waves, faces washed with ocean spray, all their minds racing with the engine, wondering what life would really be like here, together, in America."

"I don' need eyes to dig with a shovel," Santos shouted out in declaration. "I will dig to pay my friends for what they have done. And I must care for my bride!" He winked at Willie. "You will be the best man, yes?"

"You sly dog," said Willie. "You betcha, yes!" He leaned in to whisper into Santos' ear, though it came out as a shouted declaration, "And she's every bit as special as you said she was!"

Marcella cast her eyes down shyly and quickly changed the subject. "When will we be able to see the rock that made you so famous? Is it close to where we will get off the boat?"

Santos smiled and reached an arm out to drape over her shoulders. "It was there when we left, watching us go, I believe," he said. "I am sure it will still be there, waiting for us all to arrive."

"Well, we ain't exactly headin' that way," Willie shouted over the boat's powerful motor.

"No? Santos asked in surprise.

"Oh, please, Willie, we would like to see the rock that Santos made to look like the American eagle," Mama' implored. "I would like to check on my old friend myself, "Santos added," to be sure that no one has moved it in protest or damaged the work that has been accomplished, since I will do no more. Please, Willie, you will take us back to the beach we departed from, yes?"

Willie looked at his watch, then shook his head. "Nope. Can't do it. We'd get off schedule."

"Off schedule?" laughed Santos. "Like we got the big important place to be! Sand Harbor is where we are heading, is it not?"

"Well, yeah, eventually, but this captain's headin' for the pier that's a ways from that beach," said Willie. "He's gotta get this cruiser back to dock. But you could take a quick look over yonder as we go by," he offered casually, gesturing a big wave in Sand Harbor's direction as they flew past it. Noting the obvious disappointment on his passengers' faces, he added, "You'll have plenty o' time to visit with Ol' Wings Jr., don't you worry!"

Santos nodded, trying to erase all traces of sadness from his face. Everyone else fell silent for a long moment. Then Marcella leaned into Santos and offered cheerily, "Ahhh, but we are free, really free, and we are here with you!"

"Yes," affirmed Mama'.

"*Si, si,* it is really the true thing that happens to us," said Papa'.

They were all obviously making a very brave effort at being cheerful for deeper reasons than Santos' artwork. For so long, they had wished for escape, but now, they had to reckon with the searing pain of finality, of being separated from their homeland, perhaps forever. They had to quell the rushing question again and again: would they ever see the lush beauty of their Cuba again? Would their beloved country ever be free again? And could they send for Marcella's family soon? This, Marcella couldn't stop wondering.

At first, the Latin music was such a natural blend for their thoughts they hardly noticed it until it was blasting at them from just around the bend.

"Someone is celebratin' somethin'," said Santos. "Sounds like a very big party."

"Maybe we can get the invitation!" said Papa', grinning so broadly for the first time that he openly displayed his missing front tooth.

"I think that can be arranged!" Willie announced as the yacht turned toward the shore and its motor was abruptly cut back.

Santos started laughing, feeling his way toward Willie. "Ha! Ha! You think we could crash the party? From the sound of the mariachi, I believe that would be a great way to welcome my little family to their new home."

Just then, a voice announced from the stand where the music was playing, "Welcome to America!"

"Yay!" a huge cheer erupted from the same location.

Santos, Marcella, Mama', and Papa' again huddled together in stunned silence, though this time they felt no fear. Only confusion and surprise.

"What is going on, Willie?" Santos demanded. "Do you know somethin' we don't?" He could sense that Willie was beaming; the others could see it clearly.

"Guess they decided to throw you a welcoming party!" Willie answered, shrugging his shoulders in a failed attempt at nonchalance.

As the yacht pulled up to the dock, the band faded out the Latin music and replaced it with a boisterous rendition of "America the Beautiful!" Santos' eyes glistened as he made his way off the yacht and stood at attention, trying to sing along with the crowd, stumbling over the words.

"What a reception the refugee is given here in America!" Mama' cried out.

"I don' believe this is the usual way," said Papa', wiping at the corner of his eye. "I am thinking this might be special for our Santos."

"Santos is very special," whispered Marcella.

"Come on, Santos, they're clappin' for you," ordered Willie, taking his friend by the elbow to guide him up along rows of newly placed concrete steps.

"How? Why? When?" was all Santos could stutter, completely overwhelmed as he made his way up the steps.

He recognized Mayor Devon's all-too-familiar voice booming out over the crowd as they made their way, Santos reaching back often to make sure Marcella, Mama', and Papa' were right behind him. "The Village of Sand Harbor is honored to welcome our new citizen-to-be, Santos Gonzales. And we welcome his family to America!"

The crowd broke out in loud applause. Mama's hand flew to her chest in utter astonishment.

The mayor cleared his throat and continued seriously, "While we are a nation of laws…" he hesitated for emphasis and looked out over the crowd in stern warning. "And we cannot thus condone or even *allow* our laws to be broken with abandon…"

Low whispers rippled across the crowd like a piano rift reaching for its crescendo.

"We are also a nation with heart," he smiled out over the crowd, as it now silenced him with applause. He cleared his throat and held up his hand. Willie kept working Santos toward the podium. "That is why America welcomes those who flee from tyranny and make it to our shores."

"Yaaaay!"

Santos recognized Al's deep voice, a loud bass drum accenting the rhythm of the long, cheering applause. He knew they would all be there, Pete and Andy, even Hank, and the rest of the crew. He was overwhelmed, but still confused, as Willie pushed him toward the podium. Before he knew it, he was standing right beside Mayor Devon, who reached out and grabbed his hand to shake it vigorously.

"We especially want to thank you, Mr. Gonzales, for reminding us how very fortunate we are to live in a free country—" He was interrupted again by a thunderous round of applause and shouts of "hip hip hooray!"

"And for your stalwart…and, I hear, rather stubborn"— he added with a wink, as laughter erupted from the familiar voices of Hank and his crew—"protection of our proud symbol of freedom, the magnificent bald eagle!"

Mayor Devon stepped sideways closer to Santos, and waved his arm toward a large figure in the center of the alcove that Santos hadn't even noticed. "Why don't you do the honors for us, Santos?" he said, pushing him forward and giving him no chance to object. "Please remove the black cloth from your masterpiece!"

Santos caught his breath, reached out, placed his hand on the mysterious object, and held it there for what seemed like a year to Marcella, Mama', and Papa'. Still confused, but now full of hope, he clutched the cloth by the corner and pulled.

"Ladies and gentlemen!" Mayor Devon announced proudly, "Americans, all! Immigrants, all! We give you Wings!" A fresh roar mushroomed up and out over the crowd, out to the beach, and up to the stage where Santos stood in amazement. Somehow, the eagle's boulder throne had been moved from the beach to the main city harbor, where people regularly boarded and disembarked from big ships. Mounted on a large concrete block at the top of the stairs, the boulder looked as if it could take off any minute. From the firm set of the head and beak to the dainty scallops and strong feathers grooved outward from the breast to point sternly from the ends of the wings, Santos had captured the eagles' likeness in minute detail, even with his limited vision. The eyes were keen and focused. A semblance of talons reached out from the boulder's base, as if prepared to clamp shut on a fish in midair.

Again, Mayor Devon had to raise his hand to still the whistles and cheers. "Most importantly," he continued, in a slight tone of admonishment, "because we must maintain our status as a nation of laws." He continued, "…and, of course, to show our appreciation for your beautiful artistic rendition of freedom, we would like to commission you, Mr. Gonzales."

Santos looked at him quizzically, turned around to search for Willie. "Commission? What does that mean, commission? Me? Am I havin' to go into the army?"

A few people close to the stage stifled a giggle. Willie came up behind him and whispered, "It means they want to *hire* you."

"Hire me?"

"That means *pay* you!" Willie added too loudly as his words reverberated over the microphone. Everyone, including the mayor, laughed with approval.

"Yes!" he said. "We are going to pay you if you will complete this beautiful symbol of America's freedom you have begun, even as you have had to persevere through many difficulties."

Santos was now weeping openly, making his way down to bring Marcella, Mama', and Papa' back up to stand beside him.

"That is the American way!" Mayor Devon continued. "Not only will we pay you, Santos. We have already received requests from Braxton Harbor and Eden Bay for their own "Wings" by Santos Gonzales, and that's just the beginning."

Santos turned around to envelope his loved ones and reached out in search of Willie's strong arm to squeeze it in gratitude.

"And now," announced the mayor, "we have asked your good friend, Willie, to read aloud for you and the good people gathered here before us the plaque we have had made for your eagle. Willie?"

Willie cleared his throat ceremoniously, stepped up to the microphone, and held the plaque up for all to see before turning it to read with a trembling voice,

All who love Freedom, who yearn to Be all you are meant to Be
Welcome to America's shores.
Come. Live with us. Love with us. Work with us
In Freedom's land and skies.
Believe and Be Everything
You Can Be.
You are tomorrow's Feathers in America's Wings.
Lift your own Wings, for they are Significant to us All.
Together we Form. Together we Lift. Together we Fly
On the Wings of Freedom.
On the Wings of America.
On Mighty Wings of Significance.

Santos pulled his loved ones close. They were not alone as they all wiped at their eyes. Santos was sure he heard the boulder crying out to the universe, "Whhhhheeeee! My purpose is once again grand! I truly am, at this very moment, and forever, all that I was meant to be!"

The waves whispered, whooshed, whispered, whooshed, "Forever, forever, forever, Forever! Forever, forever, forever, Forever!" Sprinkling the harbor with their mist, they sent forth a haze up, up, and gathered into white puffs high above. The truth of their song floated its fullness into the air. Time stood hushed and unmoving, yet ran shouting into forever. All was constant, yet changing; new, yet old, beginning, and ending, in the whisk of each moment. Everything seemed to stand alone. But everything was forever entwined.

On a distant island, the call to lift off abruptly and soar toward the highest clouds right at this moment of calm and serenity was no less a surprise to Wings and Mama Eagle than to all those around them. They had no need to fill their crop or search for food for their young, no distant island drawing them ever toward it, no challenge or threat to meet head-on. They only knew that visions of men tossing food in the air, of Wings springing up from a gold-flecked boulder that sat on the side of the mountain mother replayed in their minds as they spread their massive wings open wide and sped upward, high in the air at a sharp angle.

Suddenly, they split the air between them and let themselves fall backward, forming an invisible heart in the air, then curling up again and again, in a magic ballet, swimming through the azure depths in a magnificent display of strength and grace. All their senses were singing out, awakened by an incredible joy they did not completely understand. They only knew that they could fly in total freedom, and had to at this very significant moment.